MOON & SHADOW

The Channeler Trilogy Book One

J. Steven Lamperti

ISBN-13 : 978-1734597400

Lamprey Publishing
LampreyPublishing@gmail.com

Cover titles and frame by James, GoOnWrite.com

Printed in the United States of America

The Channeler Trilogy

Moon & Shadow
Sun & Dream
Death & Dragon

The Tales of Liamec

The Wolf's Tooth
By the Sea
Twilight's Fall
The Channeler Trilogy
Sunshine over Hero
The Pirates of Meara
Endymion and the Fae

For Andrea,
Who heard every word
before anyone else did.

1

There was a young man in the village, Sebastian, who went out late one evening when the moon was full, took the moon down from the sky, and hung it over the mantelpiece in his home. He didn't try to do this in secret; he didn't hide what he was doing from the other villagers. He simply did it, like he was bringing the cows home for the evening, as he had earlier.

Now in those days, people were more likely to believe things. They were more likely to believe things they saw, they were more likely to believe things they felt, and they were more likely to believe things they heard. So when a couple of villagers who saw Sebastian do this described what they had seen in the village pub, they weren't greeted with disdain and denial. Instead, they were greeted with wonder and fascination, followed by disdain and denial.

"I saw it," said one older gentleman while dunking his cheese bread into his tankard of ale. "Our Sebastian is tall, but he couldn't quite reach, so I watched him climb up onto Swenson's fence out in his cow pasture and try to grab it. Still, he couldn't reach, so he climbed up completely onto the fence and jumped. He caught the edge and swung out on it until it detached. Then Sebastian and the moon fell into Swenson's pasture. I was thinking then that he had barely missed a cow patty. And a good thing too 'cause when he came away carrying the moon, I thought it was just about the prettiest thing I had ever seen, and I wouldn't have wanted to see it all covered. If you know what I mean."

"No," said a younger man, his voice filled with disdain and denial. The expression on his face clearly showed that if the older man hadn't been dunking his cheese bread in his ale, he would have been more believable. Who does that, after all?

"No," continued the younger man, Gerard, as he swept a well-maintained cowlick off his forehead. "No one can take the moon down from the sky, and if someone could, it wouldn't be Sebastian."

There was a chorus of approval at this comment. While most everyone (except possibly Gerard) liked Sebastian, the consensus was he wasn't anyone very extraordinary. If anyone could take the moon down from the sky, it probably would be someone special. Gerard was confident in his opinion it would have been he, himself, who would have been able to do this before a nobody like Sebastian.

Sebastian was born in the village and spent his not very special youth there. The only thing anyone at the pub could think of that was even a little unusual about him was being so young and living alone in his father's house. Of course, in some ways, his father was special. He had moved to town a long time ago, with his young pregnant wife in tow and with some kind of mystery about him, something about having been a soldier. He had settled down to farming until his wife died, giving birth to Sebastian. After that, it was farming and raising his son. And until the fever took him a few years back, he hadn't given the villagers much to talk about, which was how they liked it for the most part.

The mayor, who felt he had to take charge of this conversation to assert his stamp of authority on the crowd, said, "Like father, like son. The father was some kind of big-wig soldier, and now the son thinks he can take the moon down from the sky."

The older gentleman, dismayed at how he was losing the crowd's attention and still smarting at the way Gerard had shown him such disdain and denial, spoke up.

"If you don't believe me, go outside. I bet the moon was up when most of you came into the pub. You know it should be rising, not setting. Go outside and look for it."

There was a bit of a rush outside. It was a sparklingly clear night. Seeing as the moon was no longer in the sky, the stars were taking advantage to show themselves at their best and brightest. The night sky was beautiful, the stars were shining like diamonds, but being from a small village, they all knew where the moon should be, and it was gone.

After filing back inside and muttering to themselves a bit about the disrespect the youth of today showed for the natural order, they looked at the mayor for some answers. The mayor, realizing there were upsides and downsides to being in charge, announced,

"All right. I need to talk to our young man and see what he thinks he's up to."

2

Sebastian's house was on the outskirts of the village, just barely inside the town wall. (The town wall was mainly just a fence. Some parts were a little higher, and some sections were more substantial, but much of it was just a fence like you would have around a field on a farm. The mayor liked to refer to it as the town wall, as that made him feel like the mayor of a town with a wall, not just a village with a fence.) Sebastian's father had maintained a little distance from the other villagers. Not that they minded this, as quite a few of the villagers liked to keep to themselves.

As the mayor approached Sebastian's house, he felt a little nervous. He thought about why that might be for a moment. He had known Sebastian since he was born, and Sebastian had always been a quiet and careful youth, not inclined to cause trouble or really to stand out in much of any way at all. Still, a little nervousness was perhaps called for, as the pulling down of the moon from the sky was a bit of a surprising thing. When one surprising thing was happening, others might as well.

Sebastian's house was nothing unusual for the village. There were some one-room cottages, but most homes in the town had more than one room. As one might expect from a bachelor living alone, he hadn't done much with the exterior decoration. The house was white, whitewashed rather than painted. Like most houses in the village, Sebastian's home was built of wattle and daub over a wooden frame. A few of the wealthier villagers had clay brick houses. The mayor prided himself on his.

* * *

The mayor knocked on the door, noticing an unusually bright glow coming from a window as he did so.

4

"Sebastian?" he called out.

"Come in," came a voice from behind the door.

The mayor opened the door and stepped inside. The door opened into the house's central room, with other doors opening back to the bedrooms and the kitchen. There was a hearth in the center of one wall. There, hanging just above the mantel, was the moon. It was a radiant moon. The sort you would look at and marvel at how full and beautiful and shiny it was. For those who could see him, the man in the moon's face was staring down, his mouth opened in shock. Perhaps at the fact that he was now in a house living room instead of in the night sky. The mayor thought it was the sort of moon where you would look at it and marvel at the feeling it was almost close enough to touch.

It took the mayor a moment to notice it, as the moon's presence was a little distracting, but hanging on the wall just beneath the moon was a well-polished old sword. The sort of sword a veteran of battle might keep to remind himself of his past.

Sebastian stood in the center of the room between the mayor and the moon. The light was outlining him a bit, and it surprised the mayor to notice how tall he had gotten. The mayor still had the tendency to think of him as just one of the kids running around town. Though, now that his father had died and he was a property owner, the mayor might have to start thinking of him differently.

"So, look at that," said the mayor.

"Yes," said Sebastian, looking at the moon. "It's pretty, isn't it?"

* * *

The mayor questioned Sebastian for an hour, but all he could get out of him was, "I thought it was pretty, and I wanted to hang it over the mantel." Sebastian didn't seem to have a deeper reason for what he'd done and no idea how. So with no answers which would help him with the pub crowd, the mayor decided he had to look for more expert help.

3

Lilith lived in her own small house on a hill just outside the village fence to the north of town. No one called her a witch, though that's what everyone knew she was. When the mayor knocked on her door and stepped inside, she cackled and said, "I know why you're here."

This startled the mayor for a moment, then he remembered that was also how Lilith had greeted him the last time he came in to talk to her.

When we said everyone knew Lilith was a witch, that was not entirely correct. Everyone was aware that Lilith could do and knew things they couldn't do and didn't know. If two women from the village were sitting at the bar in the pub, and one said to the other, "Eh, my John, he just isn't doing the things in the bedroom that he used." The other might reply, "Oh, only give our Lilith a shout. She's a cunning one. She'd come up with a potion or summat that'd help."

If two men from the village were leaning against the back fence looking over the cows, and one was to venture, "Bossy is not for the best today. I think she might have a touch of the bloat." The other might well reply, "Talk to the cunning woman Lilith. She helped when our grandson Ralph ate the entire pot of beans we meant to keep for the week. Don't know what she did, but she fixed him right up. Taught him a lesson as well; she did. He's been a right good lad since that day."

Lilith wasn't a witch, per se. She was the village's cunning woman. She had learned her cunning from the previous cunning woman, who recognized something in Lilith as a girl and had passed on her secrets. They were genuine, those secrets. Lilith could cure bloat. She could help with many ailments and injuries. Lilith couldn't make a potion that would make a young person fall in love with another young person. But she could produce one which would make them reconsider whether a specific person was a prospect for romance. Which, if you think about it, is in some ways more real and more difficult. She could do some other more impressive things, though she tried not to do too much when the villagers were around. The idea that all magic was wrong was not common; the idea that some magic was wrong was.

The most important thing (at least at the moment) that the previous cunning woman had passed down to Lilith was the knowledge that what she knew and what she taught was just the beginning. There was magic as far beyond what she had learned as she was beyond the magical knowledge and power of a child. Speaking of children, another thing Lilith had learned was to recognize the potential for cunning in others. There was very little in this village.

* * *

In Lilith, the mayor recognized the need he often felt himself to make sure of his position with a certain amount of facade. So, he ignored Lilith's comment about knowing why he was there. Lilith's facade extended a little beyond this comment, as the mayor well understood. Listening carefully to Lilith's cackle, you might recognize the pleasant laugh of a relatively young woman concealed beneath a little attempted senile cackle sound overlay. Lilith had also been known to try to dress the part, with hoods and a little attempted shadow lurking as well. Let's say her cunning exceeded her acting skills.

The mayor filled Lilith in on how Sebastian had pulled the moon down from the sky with no further delay. She made no attempt to disguise her excitement at the report. After she confirmed that the moon was actually missing through a convenient window, Lillith eagerly followed his request to go and try to find out more. It wasn't far from Lilith's house to Sebastian's, and anticipating the most exciting thing which had ever happened in this village, Lilith fairly flew across the distance.

* * *

Sebastian wasn't much more forthcoming to Lilith than he had been to the mayor. The mayor had a different priority than Lilith did on the two main questions they wanted answered. The questions were *Why* and *How*. The mayor was very concerned about *Why*. He had difficulty putting himself into the shoes of a young man who would go out one evening and pull the moon down from the sky. That's the kind of thing that people would talk about forever. It would be challenging to become mayor of a town when people could find something like that in your past. He didn't care so much about *How*. He knew *How* was somehow important, but he felt it was above his intellectual pay grade.

Lilith didn't give a flaming cow patty about *Why*. She understood that *Why* might be interesting to someone like the mayor. She couldn't bring herself to care about the motivations of a guileless boy like Sebastian. *How,* however, was a burning, blazing torch for her. If she could get any glimpse into *How* from Sebastian, she might be able to master some of it for herself. There were also hints from the person she had learned her cunning skills from that there were places to contact and things to do if indications of real power showed themselves in the village.

* * *

Lilith could feel the power in the room (it came off the moon in waves). Unfortunately, Sebastian was still pretty much the same innocent villager she had thought him to be. He didn't have anything helpful to say about how he had pulled the moon down from the sky.

* * *

There was nothing left but to report the lack of news to the mayor and go to bed.

4

The village of Westhavenfieldbrook was seldom referred to by name. Everyone who lived there simply called it the village, except, of course, the mayor, who refused to say anything but "town." Nestled between the Blue Mountains to the east and the Westhaven River to the village's west, it was a quiet, peaceful village. Too quiet and peaceful for some.

The village boasted a mill, a brewery, a smithy, a one-room schoolhouse, any number of small farms, and not much else. The mayor bragged about his civic improvements- the cobblestones in the market square and the town wall and gate-house. Really there wasn't too much to brag about. It was a quiet village.

Quiet, yes, but prosperous. No one went hungry in Westhavenfieldbrook. Many of the residents had houses or cottages with more than one room.

There was a brook that flowed through the village. After beginning its journey in a trickle high in the Blue Mountains, it ran through the millwheel on the east side, through the village's center, and finally into the river.

From the miller's perspective, it was an excellent thing that the mill was on the east side of town. As in many villages and towns, sanitation was an issue in Westhavenfieldbrook. By the time the brook's waters made it to the west side, you wouldn't have wanted them flowing over your millwheel.

The most prominent street, which led out of town, didn't connect directly to the main road. You could head north out of the town gate, and after half a mile or so, you would intersect with the main road, which ran from east to west. It ran east toward the blue mountains and west toward an old stone bridge over the Westhaven River. Most people traveling along the road wouldn't bother heading south to the village.

The village was very scenic. Looking west from beyond the last row of houses, you would overlook green fields with old stone walls rolling gently down to the shores of the Westhaven River.

Looking east from many places in the village, including the market square, the majestic Blue Mountains showed themselves on the horizon.

5

The following day was market day. The previous night's events had shaken people, and many were still trying to wrap their heads around what had happened. But, market day was market day, and things had to get done.

Sebastian had been planning to sell a cow on this market day. This was long in the planning. He needed some roof repairs, more than he could do himself, and selling the cow was intended to finance the job. Surprisingly, though, he found himself walking toward Main Street on his way to the square on this bright market morning without a cow in tow. Also, surprisingly, he found he wasn't going to turn around to go back and get the cow. Suddenly, the selling of the cow was not compelling for him. He found he was going to market for different reasons. He didn't know what those reasons were, but he was confident he would know them when he saw them.

Sebastian felt good as he stepped down Main Street toward the market square. The sights and sounds of people getting ready for the market surrounded him. He skipped a little as he strode down the street, kicking up a small cloud of road dust. The village's streets, even Main Street, were still dirt, in a way like the town wall was still a fence. The market square was cobbled, one of the points of pride of the mayor's tenure, but cobbling was expensive, took time, and hadn't yet been a priority on the streets.

Main Street was broader than the lanes and alleys leading off it, but it was still a narrow village lane. With carts transporting goods to the market square and early risers walking to the market, the street was crowded.

Sebastian waved to Mr. Arkwright, the blacksmith, as he loaded up a cart with worked metal objects he would bring to his booth.

Mr. Smith, the fishmonger, always had a friendly smile. It was often best, however, to maintain a little distance. The more exotic of his wares were imported, and the nearest ocean fishing ports were not very close. It was best to buy local fish from the river. His cart had a special double-wall, which was supposed to be filled with ice, but he had been finding ice hard to come by, and the best he could come up with was cold water from the mill brook.

Mr. Shepherd, the miller, was up ahead with two carts. One loaded with various-sized bags of flour and the other with different varieties of bread. It was a mark of pride in the village that they had their own mill. Unfortunately, Mr. Shepherd and his family weren't the best bakers, and their baked goods left a little to be desired. Many people in the village bought or bartered for flour and baked their own bread.

6

Mrs. Fisher, the village carpenter, led a cart pulling from a side street into Main Street. She had loaded it with beautifully worked chairs, chests, and small cabinets. Mrs. Fisher was a skillful carpenter, and the market day was her day to shine. Also shining, as far as Sebastian was concerned, was her daughter Isabel, who was supporting the load from the side.

As the cart pulled into the street, Sebastian found himself face to face with Isabel. His skipping missed a step, as perhaps did his heart.

Sebastian hadn't spoken to Isabel in years. Not since his father had died and not much before then. The closest he had come to doing more than talking to her was looking at her ponytail.

* * *

The village had a small one-room schoolhouse. Mrs. Shoemaker ran the school with a temperament of iron and a ruler that felt like steel. She had been the village school teacher since before the mayor was born. When the children were in school, they sat at wooden desks in tight rows. Moving was not tolerated, not in class. When recess was called, a flock of children would flee barefoot into the dusty school courtyard. Or perhaps you could say a horde if a group of eight to ten children could be called a horde.

While seated, Mrs. Shoemaker could monitor whether or not you moved. She could tell you off if she saw your eyes wandering, but she couldn't tell you off if you sat quietly and stared straight ahead. For years Sebastian had the desk directly behind Isabel. He stared faithfully straight forward, his eyes taking in every detail of her dark brown ponytail and the hairs on the sides of her neck that escaped that ponytail. The thought had occurred to him, more than once, that if he was one of those hairs, he wouldn't have tried to escape.

Somehow, Mrs. Shoemaker had gotten hold of some very satisfactory wooden desks with seats, a top which opened, and a built-in inkwell just above the hinge on the desktop. They were a bit worn but very serviceable. When practicing penmanship, the inkwells came in quite handy. There was another use for the inkwells, which Sebastian was familiar with. A couple of times, one of his male classmates had helped the female student seated in front of them to a new hair color by dunking her hair into the inkwell. The perfect hairstyle for the execution of this maneuver was, of course, the ponytail.

There were several reactions to this, only slightly different each time. Mrs. Shoemaker, of course, would implement the harshest punishment she could. This was some combination of smacks with the steel ruler, sitting in the corner with the dunce cap on, and an extended period of social disgrace. The other children, especially the other boys, seemed to accord the lawbreaker a new measure of respect. But the most significant reaction, and the one which weighed most heavily on Sebastian's awareness, was the reaction of the girl in question to the perpetrator of the act. Was it an act of ultimate disrespect, or was it an act of ultimate love?

Sebastian had spent several years pondering this question. If there was any way of knowing that ponytail dunking would have been taken as something positive, nothing would have stopped him from doing it.

7

Sebastian almost cried when he looked at Isabel on this bright market day morning. She had cut her hair. The new hairstyle was fetching, but the ponytail was gone. She was moving so quickly that he nearly ran into her.

* * *

Sebastian and Isabel both came to a stop, facing each other.

Here is where the little dance we all do when running into someone starts. Both stop; One moves left as the other moves right. Embarrassed smile, one moves right, as the other steps left. Eventually, it gets disentangled. That's not what happened here.

Isabel looked up at Sebastian. For a moment, she wondered who this tall, confident-looking young man was, then she recognized him. *Of course, it's just Sebastian*, Isabel thought. She started to smile and step past him, but he didn't move meekly out of the way as she expected.

"I'm sorry, Isabel. I wouldn't ask this of you if it wasn't important," he said.

Isabel nodded uncertainly, not sure what he was asking.

Then Sebastian did something rather unexpected; he knelt in the dusty road at Isabel's feet. She thought he was proposing for a moment and didn't know what to think of that. But instead, he reached out and took a firm grip on her right ankle. The grip wasn't hard enough to make her fall, but the unexpected nature of the contact made her lose her balance. She slipped backward, and with a small flurry of yellow dress and white petticoats, she landed on her rear. Sebastian still had a grip on her right ankle. For a second, she thought about how strong his hands felt, then indignation filled her, and she let out a grunt of protest.

She felt an unfamiliar pulling sensation at her ankles as he seemed to do something to them. Then Sebastian stood again, offering her his right hand to help her up. There was something dark in his left hand. Perhaps a pair of dark things. They were moving around in his grip. With a scowl, she took his hand, and he pulled her back to her feet.

"This is my market-day dress," she complained.

"Sorry," Sebastian repeated, "I'll have them back to you as soon as I can." He kept hold of her hand for a moment and pressed it to his lips before releasing it.

"Them?" she said.

Sebastian turned and headed down the road in the direction of the market.

* * *

Isabel indignantly started to stride off after him to demand an explanation but found her feet weren't working right. They didn't hurt, and they looked fine, but when she tried to move them, they seemed lighter, and she felt wobbly.

Mrs. Fisher came over to her.

"Isabel, are you all right?" she said.

"Mama, my feet feel funny," Isabel said.

Mrs. Fisher gave a gasp and pointed at Isabel's shadow. As mentioned, it was a sunny morning, and Isabel's shadow was painted clearly on the road dust. That is, most of her shadow. Her shadow from head to ankle, including the shadow of her pretty, slightly-dusty, market day dress, was clearly visible. There was nothing there from the ankles down. There was a six-inch gap in her shadow from the bottoms of her feet to the tops of her ankles.

8

Sebastian continued on toward the market. It felt like a great day. He felt like he had some idea of what market day was about today. He stuffed the dark shadowy things he held in his left hand into a pocket. He started skipping again. The sunlight shone through the dust kicked up around his feet.

Gerard walked down the street toward the market square, ahead of Sebastian. If Sebastian felt good, Gerard felt great. He loved market day. There wasn't anything to sell, but that wasn't what a market day was about for him. He had a new shirt, a fine-looking thing with many glorious colors mixed in a beautiful pattern. He had a bright sunny day, and with it, the expectation of many of the fine young ladies of the town fawning over him as they often did on a market day. Gerard was even hopeful some-one from a neighboring village, or perhaps even further afield, was here for the market. It didn't happen often, but sometimes someone interesting would arrive. Gerard was eager to make sure any newcomers to the village met the right people. That, of course, meant Gerard.

A peddler had come through town a few days ago. Not an altogether unusual occurrence, they were frequent travelers on the roads. Peddlers sometimes had some cunning knowledge. Sometimes they could repair things. But, primarily, especially for Gerard, they had goods to trade. The peddler had had the shirt which Gerard was wearing. The first thought that crossed Gerard's mind when he saw it was that he needed it for market day.

The peddler had some silly patter about the shirt. "Glorious weaving," "fine eastern fabric," "colors of a peacock's feather," and other similar stuff. All Gerard thought when he saw it was how good he would look in it. If he left the top two or three buttons open, a bit of his chest hair would peek through. *The colors* are *reminiscent of a peacock's feather,* he thought, *blue and green with a touch of yellow and purple.* Shirts of more than one color were unusual in the village, and Gerard was excited to see people's reactions.

* * *

Sebastian, due to his skipping, was catching up to Gerard. Gerard turned and looked to see who was coming up behind him. His smile changed to a bit of a scowl when he saw it was Sebastian. He had never been terribly fond of Sebastian. Of course, as children, they had often been part of the same games. The village was small enough that all the children had known each other as they grew. As they got a little older, Sebastian had put a bit of a damper on Gerard's effect on the ladies. For some reason, some of them went for the quiet, respectable, modest type of presence that Sebastian offered. Of course, he had no idea how to leverage this, but the simple fact of the contrast turned some of them off of Gerard.

Also, Gerard was annoyed at Sebastian about the pulling down the moon thing. If anyone was supposed to do something that got the entire village's attention, it was supposed to be Gerard, not Sebastian. Someone who knew how to dress, not someone dressed like a beggar, or worse yet, a farmer.

Pulling the moon down from the sky, what was that? Gerard thought, *An attention-getting move if I ever heard of one.* Gerard wished he had thought of it first.

Sebastian stepped up beside Gerard, clapped him on the shoulder, and directly met his gaze. Gerard was a little taken aback at this. As part of the whole modesty act, Sebastian usually let Gerard control the eye contact when they interacted.

"Gerard, if it's not too much trouble, I would like to borrow your shirt," Sebastian said.

More than a little taken aback, Gerard was astonished to find himself starting to take off his shirt. *Why am I doing this?* He thought. *Sebastian can't tell me what to do.*

Perhaps to justify the shirt removal to himself, Gerard

thought, *It is a bit warm. The shirtless look always works for me, anyway. Didn't I see Isabel back there a little way? It wouldn't hurt for her to see my chest.*

His hands got stuck a little in the sleeves, and he felt Sebastian reach out to help him. He felt an unfamiliar pulling sensation in his chest like something was being tugged out of him, along with his shirt being pulled off. Then he stood next to Sebastian, who held his beautiful new shirt in his hands.

"Thank you, Gerard," said Sebastian. "I'll give it back as soon as I can." He turned away to start walking down the road.

Gerard felt empty. As if he had lost something.

"Wait, Sebastian," he said. He was surprised to feel tears starting to form in his eyes. "What do I do now?"

"You'll be all right, Gerard," Sebastian said. "Just try to think about what you *want* to do."

Sebastian headed on down toward the market and started whistling as he kicked up a little more sunshine and dust with a skip.

* * *

Gerard stood for a moment in the middle of the street. He wasn't sure he felt like going to the market anymore. He watched Sebastian skip off with his shirt and thought that the shirt was awfully bright. It seemed to glow in Sebastian's hands. It was a little much, with all those colors. He thought he might go home and find another shirt, a more modest one. And maybe, he'd take a nap.

9

Sebastian reached the market square. The market wasn't in full swing, but people were milling about, and many booths and carts were open. He felt the cobbles beneath his feet. The mayor was right to be proud of the cobbling. It helped keep the dust down and made the square feel elegant and respectable. It made the village feel more like a town.

Sebastian didn't notice, but he was drawing stares from the villagers. Most of those who weren't directly involved in the action last night had been told something about what happened by somebody. They weren't sure what to do with him, but they were very interested to see what he would do. Sebastian still had Gerard's shirt in his hands. It was too big to fit into a pocket, so he tied the sleeves around his waist. If he'd known he would be collecting stuff, he might have brought a backpack.

* * *

The town hall bordered one side of the square. It was more of a village town hall than a town town hall, but there it was. On both sides of the stairs leading to the main door were grassy areas, with a bench on each side. On the one to the left of the stairs, a small man was resting.

Leonard was the town fool. On this day, he was resting in the shade, enjoying the market's noises and sights and smells. No obligations were placed on him, and the village took care of him as best it could as a community. If he was hungry, he could ask anyone for food, and they would provide him with some of what they had. If he needed a place to sleep, someone would have a spare bed or at least a pile of hay in the corner of a barn. This wasn't an official thing, just something that had happened and continued to happen.

Mrs. Shoemaker, the schoolteacher, was at least partly responsible for Leonard's status. She was the one who despaired while trying to teach Leonard when he and Sebastian were fellow students. Leonard, Gerard, Isabel, and Sebastian were all of a similar age. Leonard and Sebastian had been friends during school times. Sebastian still thought of Leonard as his friend, though they had grown apart as they took on their adult roles in the village.

Leonard smiled as he saw Sebastian approach.

"Moon and shadow, Sebastian," he said, "Moon and shadow."

Sebastian smiled back.

"Moon and shadow, Leonard," he said. Someone must have told Leonard something about the events of last night. What he'd been told and what he understood were probably quite different. Still, Sebastian was confident his own understanding of what was going on probably wasn't much better.

Sebastian didn't feel Leonard was missing anything in terms of his intelligence, just that the way he thought and perceived the world differed from other people. It made it hard for Leonard to fit in in the village. When he was having trouble with Mrs. Shoemaker, Sebastian had tried to help. But Leonard couldn't say or do things how Mrs. Shoemaker needed him to, so it had never worked out.

"Are you enjoying the market and the morning, Leonard?" Sebastian said.

"The sun is shining through people today, Sebastian," Leonard replied.

Leonard wore homespun brown clothing, plain and functional. Today, as on most days, he wore a brown linen cap. Sebastian reached out, grasped his old friend on both sides of his head, and pulled their heads together so that they were face to face, only inches apart.

"Hey Leonard," he said, "I need to take something from you. Is that all right?"

Leonard looked startled, a little frightened, then he nodded.

Sebastian gently gripped the cap on Leonard's head. He tugged upward, and it seemed like there was effort involved in pulling the hat up. Still inches from Sebastian's, Leonard's face took on an expression that looked awestruck, like what he was seeing was something marvelous he'd never seen before. As the cap raised, something dark, gray, and cloudy was suspended between the inside of the hat and the top of Leonard's head. The gray cloud pulled out of Leonard's head and into the cap. Sebastian took a step back, hat in hand, and waited for Leonard's reaction.

Leonard rose to his feet and looked around.

"Thank you, Sebastian," he said. "I'll be seeing you."

Sebastian folded the cap in two and tucked it into his belt.

"Good luck, Leonard," he said.

Leonard started walking briskly away, heading down a side street. He was leaving the market square as quickly as he could. He took one look behind himself and sped up a bit as if fleeing from something.

10

Sebastian looked around himself and realized he and Leonard had had a bit of an audience. The village children usually took advantage of market day to travel around the square as a group, looking for fun and minor trouble. It hadn't been so long since Sebastian, Isabel, Leonard, Gerard, and their peers had done the same. Some children were hiding behind a tree on the other side of the town hall stairs. There were several watching from the edge of the cobbles of the square. A few more were scattered around in other places.

Sebastian smiled to himself, clapped his hands, and called out, "Scat!"

They scattered, embarrassed to have been spotted. One boy, hiding behind the tree, tripped as he tried to run. Sebastian noticed some blood on his pant leg. Striding over to where the boy was scrambling to his feet, he called out, "Hey, you, wait!"

Sebastian continued, "What's your name?"

"Marcus," said the boy with a tremor in his voice.

Sebastian remembered now, Marcus Arkwright, the blacksmith's son.

"Hey, Marcus," he said, "what happened to your leg?"

"Old Widow Clark's dog. He's a mean old thing. We were trying to sneak by, and he bit me."

Sebastian remembered this as well. It really hadn't been so long ago since he was in Marcus's shoes. Old Widow Clark, who Sebastian thought of as Mrs. Clark, had been told by the mayor to keep her dog tied up any number of times. When the dog was loose, he terrorized the street. He had been young when Sebastian and his peers had to deal with him, but it didn't seem like age had mellowed the dog any.

"Let me see if there is anything I can do about that," Sebastian said. After offering Marcus a hand up, he headed off toward Blackbird Lane.

Blackbird Lane was where the Widow Clark had her brewery. It was a mark of pride in the village that they had a brewery. The Widow Clark's brew actually had a reputation that extended a bit beyond the town borders. Not too far, but a couple of neighboring villages bought from her in addition to the local trade. Sebastian noticed the gang of kids following him, led by Marcus. They kept a discreet distance behind him but seemed very keen to keep him in sight.

Sebastian reached Blackbird Lane. He could see the dog a little way down the street. Loose again. When Sebastian and his peers had dealt with him, they speculated that Widow Clark kept him for additional security. The further speculation was that she was rich from her product's sales, and there was wealth to guard. Sebastian tried to remember the dog's name. It was something he had always found ironic, like Pico or Tiny. Something that really didn't fit with the snarling, barking monster who had just spotted him and was charging down the lane toward him.

Sebastian's recollection was that Pico wasn't really a killer. He mostly liked to scare and enjoyed watching people run away from him. Sebastian also noticed Pico was definitely getting older. In addition to the gray flecking his muzzle, he was a step slower than Sebastian remembered. He was already panting from the effort of charging down the lane.

Sebastian sidestepped the rush, and Pico wheeled around for another pass. He was panting again but determined to show who was in charge.

As Pico rushed again, Sebastian stepped forward and reached out both hands toward the dog. One hand landed on top of Pico's head, and the other went down his throat. Pico seemed to stop in midair for a second as the hand that had gone down his throat emerged with something clenched in it. The dog dropped to one side, rolled on the ground, and started gagging. The thing in Sebastian's hand looked like a piece of leathery fabric. It was white or off-white and looked light and airy.

Pico climbed to his feet, still gagging, and started barking in indignation at Sebastian. The dog tried to bark, at least. As he opened his mouth and made all the actions that should have turned into a bark, no sound emerged. Confused by this failure, Pico tried whining, with a similar result.

Sebastian inspected the white thing in his hand for a second, with a puzzled look on his face. Then he folded it as best he could and tucked it through his belt next to Leonard's cap. Turning back to Pico, he attempted to approach, his hand outstretched, lowered a bit, to allow Pico to sniff it.

Pico stood his ground for a second, looked at the approaching hand, attempted again to bark with a similar failure to produce any sound, then turned and charged back down the lane toward home.

11

There was a small informal gathering of concerned citizens in the pub that afternoon. Convinced this was a meeting he had called, all indications otherwise aside, the mayor addressed the group. He banged his empty ale mug on the bar to get some attention.

"I know everyone is very concerned about what's going on with Sebastian," he said, "but don't worry. I've got it all under control."

The chatter he had momentarily interrupted resumed.

"Did you hear what he did to old Widow Clark's dog?" One voice said.

"Leonard's left town," someone else said.

"Leonard's left town?" came a third, "Where will he go? How can he travel?"

"Isabel's mother is worried. She says Isabel's feet still don't have any shadows."

* * *

The mayor wished for a second Gerard was with them in the pub. He sometimes appreciated how Gerard could make people listen to him. It wasn't that Gerard always said the most intelligent things. Still, they were stated with such confidence. The mayor had asked Gerard if he wanted to come to the discussion, but Gerard said he wasn't feeling up to it.

The barroom of the pub was all dark wood and beams. The ceiling was low, and the doorways even lower. When Sebastian came to the pub, which wasn't very often, he had to duck his head to enter.

Lilith chimed in. Everyone stopped talking and turned to look at her. For a second, the mayor was jealous. Then he imagined he had asked everyone to pay attention to Lilith, so that was all right.

"I still don't think Sebastian has any power of his own. What's happening is being done to, or with, or at him, not by him. On the other hand, it doesn't seem like he's being controlled by anything, so he still has his own free will. There's power flowing through and around him," Lilith said.

There was a moment of puzzled silence as the listeners tried to process and respond to this information, then the chatter resumed again.

"What do you think will happen next?"

"Should someone try to catch up to Leonard to see if he's all right?"

12

In the late afternoon, Sebastian returned to his house. There were still things to do. He had to make up for spending most of the day at the market. He stepped over to the mantel, admiring how the moonlight reflected off his father's sword. He had to change before heading out to the fields. He hadn't dressed up fancy for the market, but he hadn't worn his work clothes either. Also, he had to unload all this stuff he had collected.

He gazed at the various things stuffed into pockets or hung on his belt and, for a moment, had no idea what to do with them. Then he took the shadowy black things that he had taken from Isabel's feet out of a pocket. By the full moon's bright light, they were even darker and more substantial than they had looked under the light of day. He held them for a second, then smoothed them out with a stroking motion. They looked like just what they were, the shadows of a woman's feet. Sebastian took them and placed them on the floor a bit to the left of the mantelpiece. As they hit the floor, they took on an even more substantial look, and by the bright light of the moon, a pair of dark shadowy boots stood there.

Sebastian pulled the thing he had taken from Pico out from his belt, unfolded it, and looked at it by the moonlight. It was light and felt like a piece of fabric. White with an airy texture. It seemed like a piece of cloth woven out of wind and air. Placing the material carefully on top of the boots near the mantel, Sebastian watched as it shaped itself into a pair of trousers standing on top of the shadowy footwear.

Untying Gerard's shirt from his waist, Sebastian put it on the trousers. Hardly surprised now when it stood upright on top of the pants, he pulled Leonard's hat from his belt for the finishing touch. He put the brown cap on top of the neck opening of the shirt. Something was holding all these things up. If you looked out of the corner of your eye, it looked like a person standing guard by the mantelpiece. Sebastian didn't spend much time speculating about what held it all together. It seemed like a small thing compared to what he'd been living through recently.

After finishing his evening chores, making sure the animals were safe for the night, and securing the farm, Sebastian stepped back into his living room. The moonlight lit up the figure standing next to the mantel. Sebastian proudly thought it was like a suit of armor guarding a castle, though more colorful. The black boots, white trousers, peacock-styled shirt, and brown cap presented a look that made Sebastian smile. After taking in the sights of his living room for a moment, Sebastian sighed with satisfaction and headed to bed. He had the feeling it had been a good day.

* * *

Lilith had gone to bed early. The stress of trying to explain things to the villagers was very tiring. When strange things happened, though nothing this peculiar had ever happened before, the villagers thought of the cunning woman as the one who could help. She'd repeatedly explained that she had no more idea what was happening than they did. She'd finally gone home exhausted and dropped into a deep sleep. Her sleep had ended, with a start, just now. She sat up in bed and wiped a bead of cold sweat off her forehead. Something was coming to the village. Something bad.

13

I n addition to not having a stone wall, the village didn't really have a night watch. The mayor had set up a schedule, but it wasn't updated as often as it should be, and people had a tendency to skip out on guard duty every now and then. Because the fence which circled the town wasn't complete or maintained terribly well, the urgency of guarding the main gate didn't seem too high. There was a gate, however. Like the cobbled marketplace, it was relatively recent. It was part of the mayor's attempt to upgrade the village to a town. It was mainly wood instead of stone and iron, but it was closed and locked at night.

Tonight, in a significant victory for village security, the gate was closed, locked, and two guards were present. William and Reynard had decided to play cards. As William was on guard duty and it was a pleasant evening, they had pulled a wooden table and a pair of chairs out into the road behind the gate and were enjoying a game. When Reynard spotted some people approaching the gate, he brought them to William's attention. William grabbed the two tankards of ale sitting on the table and tried to hide them behind his chair.

It was very unusual to get unexpected visitors, especially at night. The excitement of meeting strangers was almost enough to offset the disappointment of interrupting the game. William stepped up to the gate. Putting on his most official voice, he called out, "Who goes there?"

There were five of them, though one seemed to be a child. A woman approached the gate with the child beside her. She said, "We're from the ruin of the village of Anesbury. We seek refuge. We've been traveling a long and weary way. Can you open the gate and let us in?"

William turned to Reynard and said, "Reynard, go get the

mayor and Lilith."

* * *

The woman looked dusty from the road, but none of the five seemed threatening. They all had backpacks or improvised bags as if they had fled their village with just what they could carry on their backs. The child holding the woman's hand was a little girl. She couldn't be more than ten years old. Her swollen, red eyes made it clear she had been crying, and not long ago.

* * *

William made an executive decision and opened the gate. He ushered them in. The other three, two more women and an older man, moved carefully inside. They seemed to assume the woman who had spoken first would be their spokesperson.

"If you'll have a seat," said William, "I've sent for the mayor."

"My name is Rose," said the woman who had spoken first. "Have you heard what happened to Anesbury?"

"They say in other parts of the kingdom, news travels as fast as a swift horse, but around here, it travels as fast as a lame, cranky mule," said William with a smile. Then he flushed for a second as he realized how inappropriate joking might seem to these people who had just apparently undergone something horrible.

Rose didn't seem to notice. She settled with a sigh into one of the chairs which William and Reynard had been sitting in. William felt embarrassed again. He realized he couldn't offer them much hospitality without leaving to go get someone to help. William had the feeling he shouldn't leave them here by themselves.

"Let me get some more chairs," he said, rushing off toward the gatehouse.

* * *

To William's great relief, it wasn't long before the mayor and Lilith showed up, with Reynard trailing behind them. Rose hadn't told him much, just that the girl's name was Anise, as she didn't want to have to repeat herself too many times. The other three had continued their silence as if they were in shock.

The mayor suggested they retire to the meeting room in the town hall, arrange some food and drink, and figure out where their visitors could sleep. He sent William and Reynard off to rouse people to help prepare.

After they settled at the main table in the town hall meeting room, and each of their guests had something to eat and drink in front of them, Rose told them her story.

14

Rose began, "I've lived in Anesbury my whole life. My whole family lives... lived there." For a moment, she seemed like she might break down in tears. All five of them looked exhausted. Anise was resting her head on her arm on the table. Her hair was draped over her face, so it was a little hard to tell, but from the gentle moving of her shoulders, it seemed she was sobbing quietly into the crook of her arm. The other three adults still looked shell-shocked and were content to let Rose do the talking.

"Anise is my sister's daughter. My sister and her husband were the first to see the thing coming."

Anise lifted her head at this.

"I saw it first," she said. "I was out in the field, and I saw it standing behind the fence. It was huge and looked really scary. When I saw it walk through the fence, without stopping or even slowing down, I ran to get mama and papa." At this mention of her mother and father, who obviously weren't with them, she lowered her head again, and the quiet sobbing resumed. When Anise looked up and started speaking, Lilith focused on her with a curious look on her face.

Rose continued. "It was, as Anise said, big and scary. On our journey here, when we were sharing our stories of what we saw, we took to calling it 'the beast,' so I guess I'll call it that. My sister, her husband, and Anise ran to the central square. The sun was starting to set. We had a bell tower, which was a landmark in the town. We rang it on the hour to mark the hour. Still, everyone in the village knew that it meant something was wrong if it rang twice. It hadn't rung twice in my lifetime, but if you grew up in our town, it was trained into you from an early age. There were still people in the square, so someone was there to help ring the bell.

"People came running. As I said, the bell had never rung twice before, but we all knew what it meant. Our cunning woman, Robin, arrived early and grilled my sister and brother-in-law about what they saw. We didn't have a mayor, and Robin was, for all practical purposes, the leader of the village."

The mayor felt an involuntary shiver run down his spine when he heard this.

Rose resumed her story, "Someone climbed the bell tower to see what was happening. Other people arrived who had seen the beast as well. It didn't seem to bother with roads or paths. It just walked through anything that got in its way. It headed straight toward the square. The people who were ringing the bell kept ringing it. There didn't seem to be any reason to stop.

"At this point, those of us in the square, which was most of the village by then, could hear the sounds it made as it came toward us. Crashing and crunching sounds. Louder, as it got closer than anything I've ever heard before.

"It arrived at the edge of the square and then just stopped. It stopped and stared at us expectantly like it was waiting for something. As I said, at this point, pretty much the whole village was there, and both the villagers and the beast just stood there waiting for someone to make the first move. I wish I could describe what it looked like, but I literally can't. We've talked about that, and it seems that it looked different for everyone."

"I've told you, Aunt Rose," said Anise, without lifting her head. "It was a nightmare."

"I know, Anise," said Rose, "it was. For me, at least, it must have been ten feet tall and an indeterminate gray color. It didn't have a face but somehow still had a mouth. As Anise said, a nightmare.

"That's when I saw the bravest thing I have ever seen or will ever see. As I said, it was just standing there, expecting something, and we were all frozen too, waiting to see what it would do. So Robin stepped forward, moving towards it, and tried to talk to it. I could see her gesturing and tell that she was speaking, but I couldn't hear what she was saying.

"It waited for a second, perhaps trying to see what she was doing, then advanced forward itself and just ate her. It basically just engulfed her. It somehow opened up, moved on top of her, and she was gone.

"That broke the paralysis. There were screams, and everyone started running in all different directions. It was total chaos. I lost track of my sister and brother-in-law but somehow kept hold of Anise's hand.

"I looked back over my shoulder as we were running and saw it ripping pieces out of the bell tower. The whole thing started shaking, and a little later, I saw it fall. After that, it just started attacking people and tearing down buildings. I've never seen anything like it.

"We got out of the village and just followed the first road we came across. We've been walking for days. As far as I know, we're the only survivors, though I hope others escaped in different directions.

"Nobody in our village even had a weapon, except hunting gear. There was nothing we could do."

15

The following morning, as promised, the mayor took their visitors on a tour of the village. They seemed to be feeling a bit better. The mayor thought *A good night's sleep and a good meal can work wonders. Also, the return of the feeling of everyday village life might be helping as well.*

There wasn't too much to show in the village, though the mayor didn't let that stop him. Or even, truth be told, slow him down too much.

He showed them the gate and the gatehouse in the town wall, though they had seen that last night when they came through it. It had been dark then, so they hadn't seen much. He didn't mention that the gatehouse had the town's entire armory, comprising two spears, which the night watch didn't even really know how to use. Of course, he did mention that the gatehouse and the wall were built under his tenure.

He led them on a walking tour of the entire village, including showing where the prominent citizens lived. This didn't, of course, include Sebastian's farm. However, they saw him coming into the market square from another street as they walked into the market.

Anise cried out and grabbed her aunt's arm. "That's him, Aunt Rose, that's my hero, my knight, the one I told you about!"

A little annoyed that they weren't appropriately impressed by his cobblestones, the mayor said, "That's no hero. That's just Sebastian. Something strange has been going on with him, but he's not a knight. We don't have any knights in this village, little girl."

"He *is* a knight!" said Anise. "I wished for him, then I dreamed him, then I asked him in my dream, and he said he would help me. I knew he was here. That was why we had to come to *this* village."

"Anise," said Rose, "The mayor's been kind enough to show us around town. The least we can do is be polite and listen to him." She turned to the mayor and, addressing him directly, said, "She's been having strange dreams lately. Not too surprising considering what she's been through. Please continue."

Relieved he would get the chance to talk about his cobblestones, the mayor did so.

* * *

The townsfolk settled the refugees into extra rooms and provided them with food. Rose and Anise, because there were the two of them, were offered the opportunity to move into an unoccupied cottage. The villagers were happy to help them get back up on their feet. Though the implication was if they were staying on, they would need to find a way to contribute to the local economy.

* * *

Rose had been a baker in Anesbury, and though the cottage she and Anise were in didn't have the best kitchen she had ever seen, she made do. She had to borrow the ingredients for her first baking attempt, but it was well-received, and she was able to barter loaves of bread for ingredients for her next batch. Within a few days, she had the beginnings of a business, or at least the beginning of a way to keep herself and Anise clothed and fed.

* * *

Anise, in the meantime, spent a few days getting the lay of the land. She got orientated and learned how to get from their cottage to critical places in the village. She met a few local children, but she didn't have time for them, as she was on a mission. With a bit of detective work and a little sneaking, she managed to figure out where Sebastian lived. She knew he was the hero of her dream.

She was hiding behind a bush across from Sebastian's house. When she saw him come home after bringing the cows in from the fields, she waited just a moment longer. The light from the setting sun shone across the house front as Anise got up the courage to cross over and knock on his door.

16

Sebastian opened his door. "Hello there," he said, looking down at Anise. He hadn't been very involved with the refugees or their stories. Aside from some strange looks received while walking around the village, his life had returned to routine the last few days. He didn't mind that so much, although the feeling of adventure he had had when unusual things were happening had been exciting.

Anise was nervous, but she knew what to do. She stepped forward, just over the door's threshold, and dropped to one knee. She didn't know what to do with her hands, so she folded them together in front of her.

"Hail, Sir knight," she said.

Sebastian looked startled and paused for a second before he started laughing. He held out his hand to help her up and said, "My name is Sebastian. Where did you get the idea I was a knight?" He continued, "Also, I don't think people need to kneel to knights, anyway."

"But you are a knight," Anise insisted. "You told me so yourself. You're the Knight of Moon and Shadow."

"I told you?" Sebastian said.

"In my dream. I wished for you, and then I dreamed you. You told me you were the Knight of Moon and Shadow and that you would help me."

"I can assure you," said Sebastian, with the echo of the laugh still in his voice, "that I am not a knight of any kind. By the way, even if I am not the Knight of Moon and Shadow, I still need to know your name?"

"I'm Anise," she said. She realized what was wrong. "You're not the Knight of Moon and Shadow yet," she announced.

"I'm not?" said Sebastian. "I thought I was?"

"Not yet," said Anise. "You need to have a squire, and you need to be knighted."

Anise looked into the room and saw the moon and the sword hanging over the mantel. Beside them was the stack of outlandish things Sebastian had collected. She smiled a self-satisfied smile.

"I'll be your squire," she said in a tone which brooked no discussion, "part of my job will be to help you put on your armor," and she gestured toward the stack of things.

"Armor," said Sebastian, "that's not armor, it's just some weird things I borrowed....," his voice trailed off as he realized that the way the things were piled up did make it look like an odd-looking suit of armor.

"I can help some more," said Anise. "I think I know what to do to make you the knight." She headed over towards the mantelpiece and tried to reach up toward the sword. She was quite a bit too small to reach it, but even so, as soon as he saw what she was trying to do, Sebastian interrupted.

"Careful with that. It's sharp."

* * *

Sebastian's father had taught Sebastian many things. One of the most emphasized was that a weapon should be respected and well maintained. The sword was sharp because Sebastian took it down once a week, every week, and repeated his father's ritual of cleaning, polishing, and sharpening it. He had done this ever since his father died.

Sebastian stepped over to the mantel and pulled the sword off the wall. He grabbed the sheath also and sheathed it before handing the scabbarded weapon to Anise.

"You'll have to leave it in the scabbard," he said, "it's too sharp to play with otherwise."

"I guess that'll work," said Anise uncertainly. She turned to Sebastian. "Now kneel," she commanded.

Sebastian took a knee, and Anise tried to raise the sword above his head. Even kneeling, he was too tall, or she was too short, or some combination of the two. Anise motioned for him to wait and pulled a chair over from the table. Pushing the chair in front of Sebastian, she climbed up onto it.

Anise lifted the sheathed sword as far over her head as she could. "I dub thee...," she started to say. Her speech was interrupted as her attempt to flourish the blade around in a flamboyant swing failed. She lost her balance and almost fell off the chair. After a moment of stabilization, she lifted the sword and tried again.

"I dub thee, the Knight of," and here she touched the sheathed sword to his right shoulder, "Moon and," and she carefully lifted the sword over his head and touched his left shoulder, "Shadow."

* * *

With her goal achieved, Anise was almost glowing like Sebastian's moon as she walked home. The knight from her dreams was here to protect her.

17

The following morning was bright and cheery. Lilith walked through the marketplace, enjoying the sunshine and the sounds of the village. Since they had arrived, she had wanted to talk to the refugees, the new villagers, but hadn't had time until now. She passed through the market and headed down the lane that led to Anise and Rose's new cottage.

Rose and Anise fascinated Lilith. Especially Anise, though Rose seemed interesting herself, in her own way. But Anise was setting off Lilith's cunning sense. There was something special about the girl. The way Lilith perceived a person's cunning ability differed for each person. Anise was showing something which Lilith had never seen before.

She reached the front door of the cottage and knocked. It seemed like Rose had already been doing some gardening in the few days she had been here. Newly planted rose bushes lined the path on both sides of the doorway.

"Who is it," came a voice from inside.

"It's Lilith," Lilith said with a cackle. She and Rose had met when Rose arrived and had interacted a bit since, so Lilith was sure Rose would remember her. The cackle was just insurance, playing the part of the old village cunning woman.

Rose invited her in and made some tea. The cottage kitchen, where they were sitting, smelled pleasantly of the bread Rose was baking. Rose and Anise had begun to settle in, and the kitchen looked happily lived in. Rose's baking had been going well, though it meant early mornings. People wanted fresh bread to break their fast, so bakers were busy before everyone else got up.

Handing Lilith her tea, Rose noticed her looking around and said, "Anise isn't here. She's been going out early and wandering around the village. I'm glad to see her occupied. I know she won't forget, but I want her not to be thinking about the recent past."

Lilith nodded. "I need to ask you about her."

"What do you need to know?" said Rose.

Lilith hesitated a second, weighing her words carefully.

"My mistress Evelyn, she who taught me the ways of the cunning folk, showed me how to see that which is cunning in others. I think I see something in Anise. I need to train her."

Rose hesitated as well. She dropped her voice a little, though no one other than Lilith was listening.

"She's just lost her parents," her voice broke slightly as she said this. "I need her to have some time to be normal for a while before starting anything new."

"Have you noticed anything unusual about Anise," said Lilith. "Anything about her you thought was strange as you saw her grow up?"

"Anise has always been a happy child. She seems normal to me. Imaginative and bright, but not unusual."

"Of course," said Lilith, "we'll talk about this again some other time."

Rose looked a little relieved that Lilith was not going to press the issue.

"There is one thing," she said. "She has always had strange dreams. She'd dream about some problem or worry and then dream someone was helping her solve it. That's why I didn't worry about what she was saying about your Sebastian. It was just another one of her dreams."

Lilith thanked Rose for the tea and reassured her with a comforting press of the hand as she left. She promised to be in touch in the future about the training.

* * *

That evening, just as the sun was starting to set, the beast arrived.

18

I t started just as it had in Rose's story of Anesbury. The beast appeared on the edge of the village and slowly made its way directly toward the center. Instead of traveling down roads or lanes, it walked in a straight line, crashing through everything which stood in its path.

* * *

It happened that the direction the beast took went directly toward the main gate. Reynard was on guard duty this evening. He heard the crashing noises and stood up to see if he could tell what was making them. Everyone in the village had heard some version of Rose's story by now, but Reynard was there when she arrived, and he heard her tell it directly.

In the days since the refugees arrived, Reynard had heard lots of talk about the story. Many people didn't believe it. Some people accepted parts of the story, but the idea of the "Nightmare" or the "Beast" left them skeptical.

Reynard believed. He had seen Rose's face when she was telling the story. Reynard believed, and in some ways, had been waiting for this. He thought he knew what the crashing sounds were even before seeing anything.

Reynard got one of the spears out of the gatehouse with a resigned sigh. They were kept sharp and well maintained, as what use is a poorly maintained spear. Reynard took his spear and went to stand behind the gate.

The sun was setting. The gate was closed and shut at the first trace of sunset, so it was already locked. Reynard peered through the bars of the gate. The crashing sounds were awfully close, so he was surprised he couldn't see anything yet. Then he did.

With bricks and thatch scattering everywhere, the beast

burst through the wall of a house-the house just on the other side of the street from the gate.

How to describe the indescribable. As mentioned, it looked different to each person who saw it. Perhaps it was, as Anise had said, a nightmare. Maybe it was taking something from the fears of the observer and building something fearsome for them personally.

Reynard thought for a moment about running, but he was on guard duty. He braced the spear on the dirt road behind him and kept the point aimed at the beast.

The beast hesitated for just a second, then stepped up to the closed gate and made a backhand sweeping gesture with its left arm, tentacle, or whatever it was. The motion swept the part of the fence it touched, the gate, Reynard, the spear, and the gatehouse aside like so much debris. The beast stepped forward, over the remains of the gate, and continued toward the town center. It ignored the pile of rubble to its left.

* * *

The village didn't have a bell tower as Anesbury had. But many people were gathering in the market square, anyway. The crashing sounds of the beast's arrival had alerted many to events, and others had been told. The market square was the central meeting place for the village. It was where the town hall was, and the villagers seemed to gravitate to it.

The lamps had been lit, and the sun was still not fully down, so there was enough light to see the signs of the beast's progress. It was heading right toward the market. It's not clear if the market square was actually in the center of town or if the creature somehow knew where it was, but regardless, that's where it headed.

Aside from the crashing sounds, another unavoidable racket was all the dogs in the village barking insanely. The dogs knew from the noise and the barking of the other dogs that this was their moment. Years of alertness, waking up in the middle of the night to alert their people about strange events, led to this. This crowning moment, this was their time.

Rose stood in the square, surrounded by the other villagers. Fear was flooding her mind, making her limbs feel heavy. *Not again*, she thought. She felt an absence to her right. Hadn't Anise been holding her hand? She looked around, even more panicked.

"Anise!" Rose wailed.

19

A nise pounded on Sebastian's door. Somehow he hadn't heard all the noise. The beast's progress toward the square was in the direction opposite to his house. He opened the door, and Anise dashed in.

She filled him in on what was happening. After he had some idea, Sebastian started to rush out the door. Anise stopped him.

"Sir knight," she said, "aren't you forgetting something?"

"Anise, this isn't the time for games," Sebastian said.

Anise just pointed at his father's sword over the mantel.

Sebastian hesitated a moment and then realized she was right. Even if there was no chance to do anything, there was no reason to leave a perfectly good weapon sitting on the mantelpiece of his home.

He walked over to the mantel and pulled the sword down. Sebastian accidentally bumped the moon as he reached for the sheath. His heart stopped beating. He had a feeling of great responsibility for the moon. He was just a caretaker.

The moon fell off the wall with a clatter and dropped to the floor. It looked fine, with no cracks or scratches. Sebastian knelt carefully to pick it up. As he did so, he noticed straps on the back, which was otherwise flat and black as a moonless night sky. The straps made it clear it was intended to be worn like a shield.

While Sebastian crouched, looking at the shield straps, he felt something cover his eyes. Anise had taken Gerard's shirt from the pile of things by the mantel and was trying to pull it over his head. It was easier to finish pulling it on than to fight it. He felt a surge of confidence and strength as he stood, his father's sword in one hand, the moon in the other, and Gerard's shirt on.

Sebastian laughed. He felt good. Why was he always so careful? There was nothing he couldn't do if he set his mind to it.

He took a look at the shirt he was wearing. He saw why Gerard had liked it. The colors were stunning. And why shouldn't a man try to look good if he was a good-looking man? Somehow, though it looked the same, the shirt felt thicker and more substantial than it had.

Anise handed Leonard's cap to him, and Sebastian folded it over his belt. He knew the cap was not to be worn until the right moment.

"I'll help you put on the boots, but you're going to have to put on the pants yourself," she said.

* * *

Sebastian stepped out the door of his house, followed closely by Anise.

"You said it was headed to the market square?" he said, puffing out his chest a bit, so the moonlight from his shield reflected a little better on the peacock colors of his shirt.

Anise just nodded, and the two of them set off together. Sebastian had to keep consciously slowing down to keep pace with Anise for some reason. It felt like they were moving at a snail's crawl.

* * *

Sebastian and Anise arrived at the market square from one side, just as the beast arrived from the other.

20

The beast stepped up to the edge of the square, stopping right at the beginning of the cobbles. It stood there as if it was waiting for something. The villagers were facing it, so no one saw Sebastian and Anise enter the square from the opposite side.

It momentarily crossed the mayor's mind that he should do something as the village leader. The thought crossed his mind quickly and then continued on its way. Even if he hadn't heard Rose's story, his idea of what being mayor of this village meant was cobblestones and walls, not nightmare monsters.

Isabel and her mother were standing in the crowd as well. Isabel had her hand on her mother's shoulder, partly to reassure her and partly for balance, as she was still a little shaky on her feet.

Rose was the only one who wasn't looking at the beast in the crowd. She was still frantically looking around for Anise. When she spotted her arriving at the far side of the square, her shout was loud enough to get everyone's attention.

"Anise!"

As the crowd turned at the shout, Sebastian stepped into the square. He stepped forward, his chest thrust out, the moon shield on his left arm, his father's sword strapped to his belt.

He presented a curious sight. The black boots on his feet seemed to blend into the flickering shadows. At certain moments, they looked like leather boots colored black. At other moments, it looked as if Sebastian didn't have feet at all, as if his lower legs just faded into the night shadows.

His pants, glowing as the white color reflected the light from the lamps around the square, looked sturdy yet still flexible. Something about the material made it look like you could blow it away with a breath, but it seemed substantial, anyway.

Sebastian still had Leonard's hat folded over his belt. The color combination of the hint of brown at the belt, the bright blue and purple shirt, the white pants, and the black boots might not have been a hit at a fashion show. But in the flickering light of the setting sun and the lamps, there was something very striking about it. The glow of the full moon strapped to his left forearm brought the whole appearance to an otherworldly look.

The crowd of villagers parted as he stepped forward. The beast was still standing, waiting at the other side of the square. Sebastian headed directly toward the creature through the parting crowd. Anise made as if to follow him, but Rose sprang forward and grabbed her arm.

Some of the villagers gasped as they recognized Sebastian. Some just stared with their mouths open. Sebastian sped across the square, moving more quickly than seemed possible. When he got within a certain distance of the beast, he stopped, and the two stood for a moment, facing each other.

The beast still seemed to be waiting. It stood, if stood is the right word, immobile as a rock. Rose remembered how it had behaved in Anesbury. *It's waiting for a challenger*, she thought. *It's a nightmare, and it needs a dreamer.*

* * *

As mentioned, the beast seemed to look different to each viewer. Here, it stood in front of a crowd. Each person was seeing something they feared the most. Perhaps because he stood close to it, or maybe because he was challenging it, Sebastian now saw what all the people perceived at the same time.

Sebastian's heart skipped a beat, even with the brashness he was drawing from Gerard's shirt. It was the hardest thing he ever did to pull himself together and take a step forward toward the beast.

21

The beast seemed to accept the challenge. It took a step forward as well, reared back its head, and let go a roar that shook the buildings around the market square. If they hadn't been paralyzed with fear by the spectacle before them, half the crowd would have fled at that moment. Something about that roar shook you down to your deepest fears.

Sebastian also thought about fleeing. Brashness is brashness, but it's not quite the same thing as bravery or recklessness. Though his hand was shaking, he reached down to his belt and pulled Leonard's cap out.

Hesitating for a moment, Sebastian held the cap in his hand, worried about what putting it on might do and whether he would be able to take it off. Realizing there would never be a better time, Sebastian slapped the hat onto his head.

Sebastian's confidence jumped through the stratosphere. *There was nothing to worry about here; this would be a piece of cake. The beast was history.* Sebastian straightened his back and lifted his eyes to meet the creature's gaze. He momentarily remembered the saying, "Give me an army of the foolhardy or the brave, I don't care which."

The beast pulled back its left arm/tentacle/limb and prepared to give a blow to Sebastian as it had to the gate. The crowd saw what was coming and moved collectively back to avoid the impact. When it hit, cobbles were flying everywhere, but Sebastian, or his body, was nowhere to be seen. The mayor, somewhere toward the back of the crowd, gave a despairing groan.

Abruptly, from the beast's left, Sebastian emerged from the shadows. He crouched down and lifted the moon on his left arm toward the creature. The bright light from the full moon shone into its face, and it staggered back momentarily.

Afterward, those who were there said it felt like Sebastian could disappear into one shadow and emerge from a different one.

The beast roared again, and the crowd recoiled. Sebastian seemed utterly unfazed.

He darted back between the beast and the crowd. With his movement to avoid the blow, he had left an open path from the creature to the villagers. He seemed to be trying to prevent this. The villagers gasped again when they saw how fast he was moving.

One of the villagers turned to his neighbor. "How is he moving like that? It has to be faster than old man McGinty's fastest horse. You know the one. The one who won the race at the last midsummer fair?"

"But," the neighbor replied, "did you smell that smell? Every time he moves, there's a smell like a dog's bad breath."

* * *

Sebastian stood facing the beast again. It couldn't get to the villagers without going through him. In fact, though, it didn't seem to be eager to avoid that. Going through him seemed to be precisely what it wanted to do.

Sebastian lifted his shield, seeing the glow of moonlight spilling over the beast. He reached across to his sheath and drew his father's sword.

22

The sword felt comfortable in his hand. It was the first time he had drawn it, with intent, in a real fight, but not the first time he had drawn it, not by a long shot. In addition to teaching him the importance of cleaning and maintaining a sword, his father had spent a respectable amount of time teaching him how to use one.

"Parry in four, for that attack," his father said. "Remember to use the forte, the strong section of your blade, against the weak part of his. You don't need to whack his sword out of sight. Just displace it enough so that it doesn't hit you."

In addition to fencing, the civilized sport of sword fighting, where he learned the rules, his father taught him when his opponent would break the rules and when he should as well.

"In a real fight, it's not about whose fencing is the best or who's being the most honorable. It's about who lives and who dies."

Sebastian had hated the drilling. He always told his father he would be a farmer, and he was the son of a farmer. There didn't seem to be a point. They'd trained with sticks most of the time, and he'd often told his father he felt like a fool, waving those sticks around.

"Who knows," his father had said, "maybe someday this foolish stick waving will turn out to have been a good idea."

They'd spent countless hours drilling and practicing. Much more than Sebastian was happy with. They'd mainly trained in the yard behind the house. Sebastian's father had trellises growing wine grapes there. He made a couple of barrels of wine a year from them. They would dodge back and forth between the rows of vines. The clatter and clanking of the sticks hitting against each other echoed off the trellises. Sebastian often wondered what the neighbors thought the sounds were.

Sebastian's father never talked about his past. Whenever he was asked, he'd said something about leaving the past in the past. Pressing hadn't worked and seemed to make him mad, so Sebastian learned to let it be.

Sebastian also never learned much about his mother. Like his past, talking about his wife made his father uncomfortable.

In the end, though, Sebastian's father had to admit Sebastian was getting good. If there were any fencing competitions to enter, who knew if he would have been winning them but, by the same token, who knew if he wouldn't have been.

Sebastian was almost certainly the only person in the village who knew how to use a sword or any weapon, really. The night watch's training with the spears primarily taught them which end was the pointy end.

* * *

Anyway, this is only to say when Sebastian drew his sword, it felt comfortable in his hand.

23

The beast swung one of its arms or tentacles at Sebastian. Instead of dodging the blow or fading into the shadows, Sebastian took the impact on his shield. The jolt drove him backward, but the moon bore the shock without denting or scaring.

Sebastian launched a counter-attack with his sword. He swung at the tentacle. It looked like he hit the beast, but it hardly seemed to notice. It would take a lot more than that to do any real damage.

Anise, listening to some villagers in the crowd wondering about Sebastian's unique armor, said with pride, "That's the Armor of Gifts. I dreamed it up for him. He'll have to give it back." She looked a little sad at this.

Then there came a brief period of feeling each other out. Sebastian and the beast launched attacks and counter-attacks, each trying to see how strong their opponent was, trying to learn what would be the best strategy. Here was where the creature showed itself to be more than just an animal, as it seemed to be willing to take its time and not just launch mindless attacks.

Sebastian stumbled on the edge of the broken cobblestones while taking a step backward, recovering from a lunge. His foot slipped among the cobbles. The sound was loud in the night's absolute stillness and the hushed crowd. The chorus of dogs had quieted. Either they had said all they needed to say, or something about the beast's closeness silenced them.

The creature sensed an opportunity. It charged forward and slashed at Sebastian with the edge of a tentacle that looked at that moment, razor-sharp.

Off-balance from stumbling, Sebastian partially managed to get his sword up to block the swung tentacle. He mostly blocked the blow, but the razor edge bent around the sword blade and cut into his abdomen. There was the sound of ripping fabric and the smell of blood in the air.

Sebastian gasped and retreated more quickly. He looked down at his side. There was a rip in Gerard's shirt's purple and blue fabric. There was blood on the edges of the tear, but it didn't look or feel too bad. What did feel strange to Sebastian was the change in his mind. The confidence he was drawing from the shirt, or whatever of Gerard's he took with the shirt, wasn't gone. It just felt different.

The beast was still advancing on him, and Sebastian felt the need to slow it down or make it back up to keep it away from the crowd. His side ached a little, but he didn't feel like it would be enough to hinder him.

Sebastian launched a series of attacks, and the beast backed off a little in its attempts to avoid his sword. It was the first time he got it on the defensive, and it reassured him, as it meant the beast felt like he could hurt it.

The creature came at him again and thrust with one limb. He parried and riposted. He felt his sword sink into the beast's flesh. There was a smell like rotting meat, like something dying. Sebastian tried to pull his sword back, and it caught in the creature for a moment. He felt a flash of panic, and a bead of sweat distracted him as it dripped from the back of his neck down his spine. Then the sword came free, and he was able to step back. A trickle of dark blue fluid ran down the beast's side from the wound.

The beast roared again and charged toward Sebastian, enraged by the wound. This was the moment Sebastian was waiting for. Taking advantage of the beast's momentary mindlessness, Sebastian sped into the nearest shadow and disappeared. He emerged right beside the creature. He lifted his shield, shining the moonlight full onto the creature's face, and thrust his sword deep into its side.

The beast gave another roar, with a different tone this time. The cry sounded puzzled. It was as if the creature hadn't imagined that it could lose this fight. It fell to the ground, with a crash that shook the entire village and a splash of cobblestone fragments.

Sebastian stopped for a second, breathing heavily, then the sound of the crowd of villagers' cries of delight reached him.

24

The beast's body lay on the shattered cobbles for a moment, then it started to fade. What had seemed so substantial a second ago, so solid, faded away to nothing. After a moment, Sebastian had trouble recalling what it looked like. If he'd ever known in the first place.

The villagers remembered, or at least if they didn't recall what it looked like, they didn't care. They knew that it had been there and that they were sure it would kill them all. They crowded around Sebastian, clapping him on the back, congratulating him, and praising him.

Anise tried to get through the press to talk to her knight, but too many people were around him, and she couldn't. Anise saw Isabel standing on the edge of the crowd. She was looking at Sebastian with a puzzled look on her face like she'd never seen him before.

Somebody retrieved some strips of cloth from somewhere and carefully bandaged Sebastian's injured side. At first, they tried to rip Gerard's shirt to get to the wound, but Sebastian would have none of that. He pulled the shirt up as far as possible to give them access.

Someone else talked the Widow Clark into donating a keg of beer, and the occasion seemed well on the way to turning into a party. Then, some of the villagers remembered it might not feel like a party for everyone and went off to check what had happened at the main gate.

The gate was a ruin, and both the gatehouse and gate had been swept into a pile of rubble, but imagine everyone's delight when they found Reynard after digging through the debris. There were a few broken bones, and at first, he didn't know where he was, but he was alive, and recovery was just a matter of time.

The mayor was with the people who went to check on Reynard. He was excited to see Reynard alive but not so happy to see the main gate's ruin and what was left of the gatehouse. A little later in the evening, he was seen slumped over a beer, bemoaning the state of his civic improvements. Someone tried to cheer him up by suggesting that the place where the beast had fallen would make a perfect spot for a historical marker or statue. He went over and looked. The cobbles that weren't damaged were stained with the creature's blue blood. The body was completely gone by now. He perked up a bit and was overheard muttering something about tourism.

Someone started playing some music. There were no traveling musicians in town, so it wasn't particularly good music. The villagers who could perform weren't as skilled as they might have been. Still, it was music nonetheless, adding to the party atmosphere.

At one point, Anise noticed Sebastian had managed to slip away. She wasn't sure how long he had been gone, but he wasn't in the square anymore. Avoiding Aunt Rose, who had been looking for her for a while now (Anise was sure it was to tell her it was time to get to bed), she ran off to find him.

25

Sebastian was looking through the contents of a box he pulled from under his father's bed. He had left his father's room untouched since his death, except for a bit of dusting. This box contained everything his father had kept that had been his mother's. There wasn't much in there. He opened the box because his mother had been the keeper of the family sewing kit.

When Sebastian arrived home from the market square, he first placed all the gifts, as he had started thinking of them, onto their places. Then he got dressed in more simple clothes and headed directly for this box. For some reason, the rip in Gerard's shirt was bothering him, and he felt like there was nothing more urgent.

Sebastian took the box and went to find a seat in the front room. He took the sewing kit and put it aside for the moment. There were two pieces of jewelry in the box as well. One was a locket he had seen before, which contained a tiny painted portrait of his mother. He had seen his father looking at it and crying a few times. The other was a jade pendant in the shape of a heart. He didn't know the exact story behind this piece, but his best guess was his father had given it to his mother.

Sebastian put both jewelry pieces around his neck, then got up and got Gerard's shirt from its place. He settled down and retrieved some purple thread from the sewing kit. Sitting there and mending the fabric with his mother's sewing kit made him feel close to his parents.

Sebastian's father had taught him how to sew. He wasn't particularly brilliant at it, but mending your clothes was a lot more thrifty than getting new ones.

There came a knock at the door.

"Come in," said Sebastian.

The door opened, and a breathless Anise rushed in.

"Sir Knight...," she said.

"Anise, I've said, please call me Sebastian." Sebastian had the tone of a patient person whose patience was being tested.

"Sebastian," Anise said, sounding a little uncomfortable with the name. "Why did you leave the celebration?"

He just held out the shirt with the threaded needle attached.

He resumed sewing, and Anise sat quietly and watched him for a moment. The appearance and disappearance of the needle in the fabric and the steady motion of Sebastian's hands were hypnotic. Anise felt like something was being done that was more significant than just the mending of a shirt.

"I'm almost done," he said. "With the shirt, I mean," he continued. "I know I'm not done yet with being a knight."

"I know too," said Anise.

26

The following morning Sebastian got up early. He dressed in his gifts and packed as best he could for an extended journey. Sebastian had never been on such a long trip before, and he felt very unsure about it. It helped when he got dressed, especially when he put on Gerard's shirt, but some uncertainty remained.

He wrote a note, offering the farm's produce to a fellow villager who would maintain it for him while he was gone. He had no one specific to ask, but one of his fellow villagers should welcome the offer. He planned to give the note to the town watch as he left town. Assuming that anyone was watching what was left of the gate.

Sebastian packed a backpack with the food he could find in his pantry that would travel well. He didn't know how long he would be on the road, so he packed carefully. The townsfolk usually bartered for things they needed, so Sebastian didn't have much money in coins. He put what he had into a small pouch and put it at the bottom of his pack.

It was early enough that he hoped he wouldn't run into anyone on his way to the gate. As he stepped over the threshold and closed the door, he felt a momentary pang of sorrow. This would be the longest time he would spend away from this house in his life.

Sebastian didn't run into anyone on his way to the gate, but as he approached the gatehouse ruins, he saw a group of people standing there. His first thought was he should have snuck out a different way. The fence around the town was not very secure, and there were many ways to get through. In fact, the backyard of Sebastian's house had a gate that led outside the village fence. If he hadn't been planning to give his note to whoever was on watch at the town gate, he would have gone that way.

Sebastian thought about heading back and leaving the village by another route. But they had already seen him and were heading toward him. In fact, it seemed like they were waiting for him specifically. Anise was there, and Rose. The Mayor, Isabel, and her mother. Mr. Thatcher, the farrier, was there holding the lead of a mule. There were several other people there as well.

The mayor stepped forward and announced, "Sebastian, my boy, I need to thank you again for your service to this community. When Anise told us of your quest last night, your community spirit struck me dumb. You already did so much for us by defeating that creature. To think you're still at it astonishes me. What did she call it, 'The Quest of the Dreamer'?" The mayor grabbed Sebastian's hand and pumped it up and down with an almost painful vigor.

After leaving Sebastian, Anise had gone around the night before and told everyone in the village he was planning to leave town to track down where the beast came from. "There's nothing to stop more nightmares from coming unless he tracks it down," she told them.

Several of the people waiting had prepared supplies for Sebastian to take with him on his journey. Rose had been up since before dawn baking goods intended to travel well. Besides other kinds of baked goods, she had a specialty that was a flat raisin cake with a slightly sweet breaded crust. She had prepared a bundle of these for Sebastian to take with him on the trip. Sebastian didn't have the heart to tell her he hated raisins.

After being presented with the supplies people were so generously offering him, Sebastian thought about his simple backpack. There was no way he could take a fraction of this with him. Mr. Thatcher stepped forward and handed him the lead to the mule's halter he held.

"Her name is Betsy. She's a bit moody, but she's a hard worker," he said. Betsy peered at Sebastian as he took her lead. She put both her ears back, which he hoped meant she was con-

63

sidering whether Sebastian's taking the lead was acceptable to her and not that she was about to head-butt him.

Sebastian was overcome. "This is all too much," he said. He felt a little moisture seeping into the corner of his eyes, which he resisted, as it felt like an inappropriate moment.

"Nonsense, my boy," said the mayor. He slipped a small pouch containing some coins into Sebastian's hand. "In case you run into any unforeseen expenses," he said with a wink.

With a bit of help, Sebastian distributed the supplies onto Betsy's back. Once she was loaded, Sebastian took her lead and started to head out of the village.

Anise turned to Rose. "Aunt Rose, are you sure I can't go? A squire needs to be with her knight."

"Not a chance, Anise," said Rose.

"Good luck, my lad," called out the mayor.

Isabel ran forward, and putting her hand on Sebastian's chest, she stood on tiptoes to reach up and kiss him on the cheek. The morning sun shone right through her feet.

27

Sebastian floated on air as he left the outskirts of the village. It was a beautiful day; the sun was shining; there was an open, blue, almost cloudless sky; she had kissed him. Sebastian led Betsy. She gave him a look and cocked one ear forward while putting the other one back.

"She did," he said defensively. "I think she really wanted to, too. It wasn't just because she felt sorry for me."

Betsy looked skeptical.

It *was* a beautiful day. Not too hot, with just enough of a crisp edge in the early breeze to make the morning sunshine feel pleasantly warm instead of hot.

Anise and Sebastian had agreed that the first step he needed to take would be to travel back to whatever was left of Anesbury. From there, he might be able to track the beast further back toward its origin. It didn't strike Sebastian as odd that he was taking advice from a ten-year-old. There were even more unusual things going on.

Sebastian looked to his right as he walked along the road. He admired the sweep of the blue mountains on the horizon. To his left were the fields between the lane and the Westhaven river. He wouldn't have to walk far down the path before reaching the main road. Anesbury was to the north and east of his village. He'd been given some directions as he left town, but he also knew that each of the road's intersections would be marked. A series of old stone markers were put up a long time ago. They were old but serviceable.

It was hard to imagine that just yesterday, he'd been in a battle with a nightmare. Sebastian allowed himself a moment of pride. "I really did save the village," he said quietly to himself.

"Heee Awwwwwwww!" said Betsy. It was clear to Sebastian she was thoroughly dismissing his heroism. He got a little defensive.

"I did," he said. "Imagine what could have happened if I hadn't been there?"

Betsy snorted, and Sebastian gave up. There was no use arguing. He knew mules and knew how stubborn they could be. He was just happy she was following the lead without complaint.

He reached the intersection with the main road. The signs were there-old stone markers, carved many years ago. The one pointing back down the lane he had just walked read 'Westhavenfieldbrook.' That stone was longer than those indicating the other directions. The last few letters of the name were carved more lightly than the earlier letters as if the stone-workers had gotten tired of carving.

The name 'Anesbury' was not yet on the markers, but his directions were clear. Usually, the stones were carved with two engravings, the next village's name and one of the larger towns in that direction.

Sebastian turned to the right, to the east, toward the mountains.

28

S ebastian walked all that day. (Betsy did, too, of course). The weather continued to be mild, though the balmy sunshine that was enjoyable in the morning hours became a little less pleasant later in the day.

During the hottest time of the day, Sebastian pulled off the road when he saw a shady spot near a stream, and he and Betsy took a little rest. It was cool and refreshing in the shade, and Betsy certainly appreciated a few minutes to graze on some fresh green grass by the bank of the stream. It surprised Sebastian to discover he wasn't half as tired as he thought he should be. They'd been walking for quite a while, but his legs still felt fresh and energetic. They continued as soon as he could drag Betsy away from her grassy stream bank.

* * *

Later, Sebastian looked for a spot to camp for the night when the sun started to set. He couldn't find anything as welcoming as the spot by the stream where they had stopped earlier. Still, he found a place where he could tie Betsy up, pitch the tent that he found in one of Betsy's saddlebags, and lay a fire. Sebastian unloaded the mule and tied her up near the fire. For one thing, he wanted to be able to keep an eye on her, but he also thought it would be nice to have her close.

Sebastian knew how to build a fire, and he was used to being by himself. (In fact, with Betsy's company, he was less alone than he had been since his father died). He was unaccustomed to being outside with a campfire, preparing and eating dinner under the stars.

It was a moonless night, of course, but Sebastian was the only one in the world who had a solution for that. He took the moon off of the pile of Betsy's saddlebags and leaned it up against a rock near the edge of his fire pit. Sebastian dined under the stars with an excellent lady companion, who only occasionally grunted and snorted, by the light of a beautiful, full summer moon.

Sebastian told Betsy in great detail about his feelings for Isabel. He told her what life was like, growing up in the village with Gerard, Leonard, Isabel, and their peers, for company. Sebastian told her about his doubts about this quest. He told her he had no idea what had happened the last few days and how that worried him.

Betsy grunted at the appropriate moments. She encouraged him to continue with a thoughtful ear flick when it was correct to do so. At one point, when he mentioned something particularly interesting, she gave her mule whinny, a cross between the he-haw of a donkey and the whinny of a horse. A "Heee Awwwwwwww!" sound.

Just before Sebastian retired to his tent, he told Betsy, "You're a good conversationalist. You really know how to listen."

29

Isabel was watching her mother putting the finishing touches on a cabinet. She was planing the top smooth. Isabel's mother was a perfectionist. Anyone else would have been finished already, but she saw some barely detectable flaw on the cabinet's top surface. The final step would be sanding and staining it, but that couldn't be done until everything else was exactly perfect.

Mrs. Fisher and Isabel made most of the wooden furniture for the village. Their workshop was attached to the house. It was well equipped.

Isabel was supposed to be helping. She was 'officially' apprenticed to her mother as a carpenter. Usually, Isabel was a hard worker, but this evening she seemed distracted.

"Mama," she said. "What do you think of Sebastian?"

Mrs. Fisher grunted. Perhaps not the most ladylike response, but appropriate for the occasion to her mind.

"You mean the fact that he stole the shadows from your feet or that he just saved us all from a horrible death?" she replied.

"No, I mean Sebastian," said Isabel. "What do you think of him? Do you think he's good-looking? Do you think he's nice? That's what I mean."

Mrs. Fisher was a widow. Isabel's father had died several years ago. It was unusual for a widow not to remarry and run her own business. But, Westhavenfieldbrook was a progressive town in its own way.

"You mean, if he were to make a pass at me, would I respond?" said Mrs. Fisher with a smile.

Before Isabel could reply, she continued, "Well, he is a good-looking young man. I always thought of him as a very nice boy when you two played together as kids. I'd be tempted, but I have to say, I think he's a bit young for me."

"No, Mama, I mean for me," Isabel said.

"Oh," said Mrs. Fisher, with an expression of mock surprise. "I didn't realize he was for you."

30

Sebastian and Betsy traveled the following day without incident. There were few other travelers on the roads, and those few didn't seem interested in talking. The weather was still clear and bright and not too hot. They passed through several intersections, but each time Sebastian's directions were enough to allow him to determine which way to go. Finally, the last set of stone markers they passed included "Anesbury" on one of the arrows.

Sebastian knew they wouldn't make it to Anesbury before dark. So as the sun began to set, he looked for a place to make camp.

* * *

The sun was getting low in the sky, and he still hadn't found a place. Sebastian had been hoping to set up camp while it was still light.

The welcome sight of a campfire off the side of the road ahead caught Sebastian's attention. Hopefully, the rules of traveler's hospitality would apply. He pulled Betsy's lead forward and headed toward the firelight.

As Sebastian entered the circle of light, he saw a large man sitting by the fire. Not large in the meaning of tall, nor excessively broad, but more in his presence. The man looked up, smiled when he saw Sebastian standing there, and waved a greeting.

Sebastian walked over, still holding Betsy's lead, smiled, and returned the greeting. He noticed the man had an enormous handlebar mustache. Some traveler's stew simmered in a pot hanging over the fire. Sebastian's stomach growled. He and Betsy had been trying to make some distance today and hadn't eaten much.

"Come join me, lad," said the man. "It seems I've made too much stew for one man to eat."

"Gladly," said Sebastian. "Let me make Betsy comfortable first."

The man nodded appreciatively and pointed towards the other side of the fire.

"My two horses are over there. Maybe somewhere near them?"

Sebastian saw a pair of horses tied to trees just outside the firelight circle on the other side. He headed off in that direction. As he got closer, he saw a wagon beyond the horses. An ornate roofed wagon painted in bright colors; a showman's wagon. The light was too dim to read the writing on the side, so he moved a little closer. "Lorenzo's Cunning Goods and Services," it read.

Sebastian found a place to tie up Betsy. Close to the two horses, but hopefully not close enough that they would bother each other. He got her some food and water, then gratefully returned to the fire and took a seat.

"You must be Lorenzo," he said.

Lorenzo laughed and replied, "Indeed. And you must be hungry." He scooped some stew from the pot into a bowl and handed it and a spoon to Sebastian.

Sebastian took a closer look at his new companion. Or, he tried to. It was challenging to look at Lorenzo without being distracted by his handlebar mustache.

It was glorious. For one thing, it was lush and thick. It also stretched out well beyond what one would have thought possible on both sides of Lorenzo's face. But these things, noteworthy as one might think them, were not the most remarkable thing. The mustache hair had been trained, or perhaps educated, into an intricate spiral on each side. *Some kind of wax?* Thought Sebastian. Even though it seemed to spin around when you gazed at it, it wasn't just the spiral; it was also the texture. The spiraling curls of hair seemed to glisten and gleam in the firelight.

Sebastian tore his gaze away. Staring was rude.

"Lorenzo, this stew is delicious."
"My friends call me Enzo."

31

Lorenzo gazed at Sebastian inquiringly. "So what brings a young man like you out to the middle of nowhere like this?" he said. The spirals on the ends of his mustache moved up and down as Enzo spoke. When he ended the question, they rose with the pitch of his voice.

"I'm on a quest," said Sebastian. He wasn't sure if he was ashamed to say it like that or proud, but it felt like it would be letting Anise down if he didn't do things the right way.

"A quest!" said Lorenzo. "I haven't met a young person on a quest in a month of Sundays. That's very exciting!"

"My name's Sebastian, by the way," said Sebastian. "What are Cunning goods and services?"

"Well," said Enzo, "that's a question with a potentially involved answer. How much time do you have?"

Sebastian looked a little puzzled. "I guess I've got all night," he said.

Enzo laughed. "That was a rhetorical question," he said. "Cunning goods and services are the goods and services a traveling cunning man or woman might sell or provide."

"So, you sell stuff," said Sebastian.

"Exactly," replied Enzo with another laugh. "You have a very precise way of cutting through the garbage, don't you?"

"Do you sell snake oil?"

It was Lorenzo's turn to look puzzled.

"I suppose I do. I have a couple of different things I sell that you might call snake oil. I have an oil-based potion I brew that is supposed to be useful for repelling snakes. I think I have a formula somewhere for a potion intended to turn someone into a snake on the more expensive side of things. I haven't actually tried brewing that one before, and I'm not sure I have all the ingredients, but I could give it a try if you need it."

"Oh, I don't need it," said Sebastian. "It's just my father used to talk about snake oil salesmen, and I was wondering if you were one."

Enzo looked surprised for a second, then he started laughing again. "Oh, you are a gem, aren't you?" he said.

Sebastian wasn't sure if this was a compliment or an insult, so he decided to ignore it.

"So," he said, "tell me more about cunning goods and services."

"Well," said Enzo, "I have some expertise with alchemy, so a lot of what I sell on the goods front is potions, but I was always best at elements, so that's a lot of the services. I was never much of a channeler or illusionist, so I mostly leave those for other people. I provide a bit of stonework, plumbing work, and chimney sweeping. It's amazing how useful elemental magic is for household maintenance. I can do a moderately good controlled burn if you need a field or some brush cleared."

Sebastian had a sudden thought. He wasn't sure how relevant it was, but he didn't want to forget it.

"Do you like raisins?" he said.

It occurred to Lorenzo that if laughter really was the best medicine, then Sebastian would be an excellent tonic for his health. He laughed again.

"Love them," he said.

Sebastian got up and walked over to his saddlebags. He walked by the back of Lorenzo's wagon as he reached the bags. There were rows of little bottles on shelves inside the open back wagon door. *It makes sense*, Sebastian thought. *He needs to use every square inch of the inside of the wagon.* He read the label on one of the bottles before grabbing the package containing Rose's raisin pastries from one of his saddlebags.

He sat back down at the fire and tossed the package of raisin pastries to Enzo.

"Everyone says these are great, but I don't like raisins," he said.

"My good fortune," said Enzo. He pulled one of the pastries out of the package and took a bite. "They *are* good," he said with a smile.

Sebastian thought of the rack he'd seen on the back of Lorenzo's cart.

"I saw the bottles on your wagon. One I saw was labeled 'Grains of paradise.' Are those potion ingredients?"

"No, that's only my spice cabinet. I was using it for the stew. I'll give you a tour of the wagon tomorrow when there's some light if you want," said Enzo.

Sebastian made the mistake of looking at Enzo's face again. His eyes were drawn irresistibly to the swirling glistening spirals of Enzo's mustache.

Enzo saw where Sebastian was looking.

"You know, when I pull into a village, driving this wagon, the villagers all expect a show. I try to oblige. I use the back of the cart as a stage and describe my goods and services. They want a show, so I do some magic. You know, sparks and small bursts of flame, little clouds of smoke, levitating pebbles, stuff like that. As I said, I'm not much of an illusionist, but after I'm done with the elemental tricks, I do a few small illusions.

"The stache helps. I've enchanted it with a couple of little spells of my own invention. I bet you've noticed it seems to glisten a bit. That's water magic. The spiral effect is a combination of illusion and air. If people spend enough time looking at my mustache, they don't notice any flaws in my performance. Also, it makes 'um more interested in coming to talk to me about my goods and services.

"Anyway," said Enzo. "That's enough of me talking. It's your turn. Tell me about your quest!"

32

Before Sebastian could respond, Enzo continued, "And this story better include a complete description of why you're dressed like that. Gotta be the most interesting outfit I've seen since I saw my first girlfriend in her birthday suit."

Sebastian was wearing Gerard's shirt, his white leather trousers, and the shadow boots. He also had his father's sword at his waist. It felt like it was right to wear it, though he wasn't expecting to need to use it on the road. The road in these parts was usually safe. Leonard's cap was in the same saddlebag as the moon.

Sebastian told Enzo his story. He couldn't think of a reason he shouldn't. It took a while. Lorenzo had to get up to put a new log on the fire at one point. Sebastian noticed he had quite a pile of firewood. He wondered momentarily if Lorenzo had collected it at this site or if he kept it in his wagon.

Lorenzo looked thoughtful for a bit after Sebastian finished.

"That's quite a story, son," he said finally. "I would call you a liar except for a couple of things. For one thing, everyone's been talking about the missing moon for days. And for another, after our conversation of this evening, I don't think you're even capable of lying."

Lorenzo mumbled a few words under his breath and made a quick hand gesture. He reached out and put his hand lightly on the white fabric of Sebastian's trousers. "Also," he said, "I'm surprised I didn't feel all that power. I must be getting old."

"I am *so* capable of lying!" said Sebastian indignantly.

"Not sure that's the most important take-home message from what I said," said Enzo.

Enzo leaned back a bit and gazed at Sebastian thought-fully. "Son, it sounds like you got yourself caught up in the middle of a powerful channeler battle."

"Channeler. I heard you use that word before. What's a channeler?"

Enzo grunted in disbelief.

"My word, what are they teaching these kids in school nowadays?"

"The teacher at our school didn't think much of magic," said Sebastian. "She wouldn't talk about it and didn't like it when we did."

"Primitive," said Enzo. "Well, if you're interested, I could fix one mistake she made in your education."

Sebastian looked around at their surroundings and re-plied, "There's not much else going on. Go ahead."

Enzo looked pleased and settled himself a little before starting. It occurred to Sebastian that salespeople and teachers had one thing in common. Both of them liked to hear themselves speak.

"I'm sure you know the difference between us cunning folk and those who call themselves mages. But to summarize, the biggest difference is that we cunning folk teach each other out here in the real world. Mages all learn at the magic academy." Here Enzo waved off in a vaguely northwestern direction.

"They're arrogant. They don't believe anyone who hasn't studied at their precious academy can do real magic." Enzo looked genuinely angry about this, though Sebastian felt he saw some hurt in his expression.

"Anyway, at their academy, in addition to training stu-dents to become mages, they do research, write papers, things like that. One thing they've done is to categorize magic into spe-cific disciplines, and they train people in those areas. The four main specialties they define are; elemental magic, alchemy, illu-sion, and channeling.

"There are those of us who think they missed a couple. There are debates within the academy as well. For example, people specializing in healing would like the academy to have a healing discipline. They use some alchemy, channeling, and elements in their magic. Still, the sum of the whole could be thought of as a new discipline. There are others like that.

"Elemental magic controls and uses the four elements: earth, air, wind, and fire. Alchemy is the mixing and enchanting of potions. Illusion magic is the discipline that allows the creation of illusions. Things that fool the senses but don't really exist. Finally, channeling, the one we're really interested in, is the conjuration and control of powerful magic spirits."

Sebastian reconsidered and reached over to the open package of raisin pastries and picked one up. He took a bite.

"Actually," he said, "these aren't too bad."

Enzo grabbed the package and pulled it closer to himself.

"No," he said with a wink, "Mine.

"But to continue, as I was so rudely interrupted. Channeling is interesting because it's indirect. Each of the other disciplines I listed allows direct control over the spell you're casting or the thing you're creating. In the case of channeling, the mechanism involves non-conscious thought.

"In its most uncomplicated form, a channeler dreams about something they want to happen. The wish is sent to the dreaming world, and a spirit may respond by coming to our realm and attempting to make the dream a reality. Sometimes the spirit comes here directly. Other times it controls animals, people, or things in this world.

"The complexities of channeling are many. For one thing, unless trained, people don't have control over their dreams. It also isn't immediate. The dreamer makes the request to the spirit world, and then the response may or may not happen sometime later.

"As I said, I have never been much of a channeler myself. The closest I ever came was one time when I dreamt some squirrels were storing their nuts in my spice cabinet, and when I woke up, I found them trying to get in through a window.

"That brings us to your situation. I think your nightmare

is an attack by one powerful channeler and what's happening to you is a defense by another. I'm afraid I don't know any more about it than that, and that's just a guess, but I would call it an educated guess."

33

L ilith caught up to Anise just as she was leaving the clearing where the gatehouse had been. Not that there was much of the gatehouse, or the main gate, remaining. They had just started rebuilding. Lilith found out from Rose that Anise asked every day to see if the watch had heard from Sebastian.

"Anise," Lilith called out. Anise turned and waited for her.

"I wanted to ask you," Lilith said, "about the Knight of Moon and Shadow."

Lilith had decided this would be a better way to get Anise talking than to ask her anything about herself.

It seemed as if it might work. Anise perked up as soon as she heard the name.

"What do you want to know about the Knight?" said Anise. Her tone conveyed that she thought Lilith had come to the right source for the information.

"Tell me about his armor," Lilith said.

Anise was very excited to talk about the knight's armor. She had named each piece. There were the Shadow Boots, the Pants of the Wind, the Fool's Cap, and finally, the Tunic of the Peacock. The moon was just called the moon, and Sebastian's sword didn't really have a name. She told Lilith about each piece in great detail.

"He hasn't come back yet," she said sadly. "I think it'll still be a while."

"Did you say you dreamt about the Knight?" said Lilith.

"I dreamt him, and I wished for him. No, I mean I wished for him, and then I dreamt him," said Anise.

Anise started fidgeting, and it was clear to Lilith she was eager to leave.

"One more thing, Anise," she said. "Do you have other dreams which are real?"

"All my dreams are real," said Anise. Her expression made it clear this should be obvious.

Anise ran off, calling out in an attempt to be polite, "Sorry, I have to go."

34

I n the morning, Lorenzo remembered his promise to show Sebastian the inside of his wagon. Sebastian found the tour fascinating. The potion ingredients were quite interesting, but Lorenzo's collection of magical artifacts was even more absorbing. Lorenzo had a small selection of items that had somehow gained permanent magical properties. He kept them near his desk/workbench, where he worked on developing potions and spells.

"Permanent enchantments on items are rare," Enzo told Sebastian. "Most spell effects are temporary, and the process of making them permanent isn't well known.

"That's one of the debates at the magic academy, by the way. There used to be a discipline called crafting, which studied creating permanent magical items. Most of that knowledge has been lost."

Enzo had a small silver ring, which made Sebastian feel warm all over when he put it on. Enzo told him it would keep him warm even if it was freezing outside and he was naked. There was a small clockwork bird that sang and flew around the room when wound up. Enzo said he supposed it might be possible to make such a thing without magic. The windup mechanism controlled the spell and was mainly used as a timer to determine how long the bird would fly and sing. It sang beautifully and seemed to be able to avoid bumping into things as it flew around the inside of Enzo's wagon.

At this point, Enzo asked if he could see the other things Sebastian had told him about over the fire last night. He was intrigued by the moon and wanted to see Leonard's cap.

"You know," he said, while admiring the moon, "there are two different ways enchanted items can come into existence.

"Crafting, as I was saying, is the art of making spells and magical effects permanent. It's mostly lost, though there are hints and indications people used to know more about it than they do now. But the other main way items can become enchanted is through channeling. After the spirit summoned by a channeler leaves the world, the things they do here can persist. If you were to give away, keep, or sell these items you have, they would most likely keep their magical properties."

"They were gifts! I have to return them," Sebastian said, shocked at the suggestion.

"Oh, I'm not suggesting you should," said Enzo, smiling. "I'm just telling you what would happen if you did. You are, at the moment, a walking treasure trove of magic. It would be best if you were a little careful. Not everyone out here is as good-hearted as I."

After the tour was over, Sebastian thanked Lorenzo for his hospitality of the previous night. Sebastian was heading into Anesbury, and Lorenzo was going the other way.

Lorenzo had been through Anesbury the day before and told Sebastian a little about what he saw there.

"I didn't spend much time looking around, as there wasn't much to see," he said, "the town looks like it's been flattened. I didn't even see anyone trying to rebuild. Nothing dangerous to warn you about, but on the other hand, like I said, nothing positive to look for either."

Lorenzo wished Sebastian good luck on his quest and headed off. Sebastian and Betsy traveled on to Anesbury.

35

A nesbury was both worse and better than Sebastian expected. It really had been flattened. There was hardly a beam or piece of a wall standing above the ground. It was as if the beast had gone through each building and knocked over every structure and standing timber.

On the other hand, there weren't any bodies. After Rose's story and the beast's actions in Westhavenfieldbrook, Sebastian expected to see dead villagers. It relieved him that he didn't.

Anesbury had been about the same size as Sebastian's village. Maybe a little bigger.

Sebastian and Betsy didn't run into anyone as they walked into the ruined village, so Sebastian headed toward the central square where Rose had said the bell tower stood.

In addition to not seeing any people, there didn't seem to be any signs of reconstruction. Perhaps any survivors had given up because of how much damage the beast had done. Or maybe they hadn't yet returned to the village.

The feeling of the ruined village was ominous. Sebastian felt the hairs on the back of his neck stand up. It was morning and a bit overcast. The feeling Sebastian had didn't have anything to do with the weather. Betsy had both of her ears plastered back on her head. In the last couple of days, Sebastian had figured out that this meant she was seriously considering refusing to do something. She was still following the lead for the moment.

Sebastian and Betsy stepped into what had been the main square. The bell tower's ruins were on the other side of the space from where they were standing. Between them and the tower ruins were six recent graves. A simple wooden unnamed grave marker was positioned at the head of each pile of earth. An enormous pitch-black raven was perched on the first of the wooden signs.

Betsy balked and nickered fearfully. Standing just on the other side of the graves was a man dressed in black. He was a little shorter than Sebastian. He had his arms folded, and he was leaning on a shovel stuck into the dirt mound of one of the graves. His face was hidden behind the black-dyed cap he had pulled down almost over his eyes.

Sebastian was momentarily relieved to see someone but changed his mind as he looked at the man. Betsy absolutely refused to move any closer. Sebastian tied her lead to a broken and burned section of timber. After the beast had destroyed the village, fires had started.

He headed over toward the man. It was hard to tell with the cap pulled over his eyes, but it seemed he watched Sebastian's every move. As Sebastian started into the square, the raven on the first grave marker spread its wings and cawed as it flew away.

"Good day to you," said Sebastian.

The man grunted. As he got closer, the man looked even more unusual to Sebastian. His black clothing was one piece; there didn't seem to be a division between the pants and the shirt. He kept his head tilted down, so Sebastian couldn't see his face.

"Do you know what happened here?" said Sebastian. "Are there other survivors?"

"I'm a caretaker," said the man. His voice rasped, a little like a chain dragged over a washboard. "There were three of us; the others have moved on. I stayed behind in case other things needed to be done. He tasked us with cleaning up."

"There was a creature, a beast," said Sebastian. "Do you know which direction it came from?"

The man waved to the northeast.

* * *

Try as he might, Sebastian couldn't get anything else out of him. He untied Betsy and led her around the square. She refused to go through it. They made their way to the northeast corner of the village. They found the remains of a farm, which Sebastian speculated was Anise's parents', where the beast first entered the town.

There was a trail leaving the village in more or less the right direction. Sebastian had no better plan than to track the beast back to where it came from, so he and Betsy followed the trail out of town.

36

Mr. Shepherd, the miller, was waxing eloquent on the subject. He was grinding the words like his mill ground wheat. "She just moved to town, and suddenly she thinks she's in charge of making bread for everyone?"

Sitting a little way down the bar, the mayor perked up at hearing the word "town."

"My family has been making bread for the folk of this village for ten years," the miller continued. "We don't need two bakers in a village this small."

The mayor sagged back down and sadly took a sip from his ale mug.

There was a muttering from the group. It seemed they agreed with part of what the miller was saying. Specifically, there didn't need to be two bakers in the village.

"As I said, we've been making bread for the village for years. We make great bread!"

The muttering seemed to be veering toward the skeptical.

Mr. Smith, the fishmonger, rose to his feet. In the evening, at the pub, the respectful distance people kept from him during the day was waived. After an ale or two, the fishy aroma which seemed to cling to him was less bothersome.

"Byram, you know we all love you," he said as he clapped the miller on the shoulder. "But your family bakes bread that tastes like boiled leather."

There was a chorus of positive responses when this was said. It seemed to have struck a chord with the group.

"Earwax," said one voice from the crowd.

"Toe cheese?" said another.

"I'd rather eat the boiled leather," said a third.

Mr. Smith interrupted before the chorus could get completely out of hand.

"Byram, maybe it's all right that someone else is doing the baking. You and yours still mill all the flour."

Byram didn't look particularly happy at this. Still, he sensed the crowd's mood was against him and decided to fight this battle another day. He sat back down on his barstool and pulled his ale mug closer.

37

Sebastian and Betsy were some ways northeast of Anesbury. They'd been following the road, as it was heading in mostly the right direction. The evening came on, so Sebastian found a place to camp. He was worried about their aimlessness.

Anesbury had been a clear destination, but now it felt like they were lost. Despite his concerns, there was nothing he could do about it until morning. Sebastian tied Betsy up and provided for her. He set up the tent so thoughtfully given to him as he left the village, and he started trying to cook something over the fire.

The sun was setting over the mountains in the east. Sebastian had never been this close to the mountains. His whole life, they'd stood off in the distance; majestic, unapproachable. Now it felt like they were very close. In fact, people probably considered the hills rising to the east of the road he and Betsy were traveling to be part of the foothills of the Blue Mountains.

"Ho, the traveler!" came a voice from over toward the road.

Sebastian looked and saw a worn-looking wanderer heading toward him.

"Ho," he called out.

"Need any company?" said the man as he approached.

"Feel free to join me," said Sebastian. He looked over the man as he unloaded the most massive pack Sebastian had ever seen. It seemed to Sebastian the wanderer was a traveling peddler. Sebastian was surprised he didn't have a horse or other pack animal with him, but from the ease with which he unloaded his massive pack, perhaps he didn't need one.

The peddler settled down across the fire from Sebastian. He offered to help with the cooking. Sebastian gratefully accepted the help. He hadn't yet figured out the details of cooking over an open fire.

As they got their food ready, Sebastian couldn't help but notice the peddler kept looking curiously at his shirt. Seeing as the peddler was already inspecting him, Sebastian did the same. The man was probably somewhere in his mid-thirties, and it seemed the road had worn him down a bit. The enormous pack had a pair of saddlebags attached to it, so the peddler had a donkey, mule, or horse at some point. Maybe the fortunes of a traveling peddler were subject to ups and downs.

His clothes were worn, and he hadn't shaved in a while. Perhaps he hadn't bathed in a time either. Though maybe the smell Sebastian was smelling was the smell of the spices being added to the meal. However, his gear looked well taken care of, and though worn, his clothes were carefully and well mended.

"I know that shirt," the peddler said. "I sold that shirt to someone not long ago."

Sebastian told the peddler about borrowing the shirt from Gerard, which led to talk of Westhavenfieldbrook and his and Betsy's journeys. The peddler let Sebastian know he'd like to hear the rest of the story over their meal.

After Sebastian had gleaned a few tips about preparing meals over an open fire and the meal was prepared, they settled back to enjoy their supper and the conversation.

The peddler told Sebastian a little about life on the open road. It fascinated Sebastian. He'd seen just enough of this life in the last few days to know he wouldn't want to live it, so he was quite interested in hearing stories from someone who did.

After telling some of his stories, the peddler turned to Sebastian.

"So, I've been sharing my stories. Why don't you share yours?"

Sebastian hesitated a moment, remembering what Enzo had cautioned him about. But the warmth of the fire and the enjoyable conversation had left him feeling very agreeable, and he decided there was nothing to worry about. It might have helped with this decision that he and the peddler had been passing a bottle of old Widow Clark's best back and forth.

Sebastian told the peddler what had happened to him since he had pulled the moon down from the sky. The peddler seemed interested and encouraged the tale with interjections and appreciative sounds from time to time.

The peddler looked thoughtful when Sebastian finished and said, "That's quite a tale, son."

After another pause, he continued, "I have a couple of things to share with you in return that you may find interesting."

"First off, I hear a lot of things in my travels. There's a story they tell in these parts which might be relevant. The local folk talk about a cave in the hills that houses a wizard hermit fellow. The hermit mostly keeps to himself, though he has to contact people occasionally for food and other supplies. The stories they tell about his cave, though, are intriguing. They call it the cave of nightmares, and no one dares go near it. They talk about horrible sounds, and there are stories of locals who entered the cave but didn't return.

"The other thing," continued the peddler, "is a story I've heard. If you're interested, I'd be glad to tell it."

"Of course," said Sebastian.

38

The peddler seemed experienced at telling stories. Perhaps it was part of what he did as he traveled around selling his wares. He sat up straight in the firelight and made a dramatic gesture as he began to recite in a sing-song voice.

"The boy who hid behind the moon." After the briefest pause to clarify that this was the story's title, the peddler continued.

"There was a village in a southwest corner of the kingdom. It was not the largest village. There was nothing particularly noteworthy about it, except that the citizens had recently come into some good fortune. Their income mainly came from mining. The village had grown up around a small gold mine. The mine was not particularly successful; it produced just enough gold to keep the citizens in their jobs.

"The stroke of good fortune they recently had was hitting a rich vein in the mine. This had changed things in the village. Suddenly there was an influx of wealth. Unfortunately, this wealth was not being evenly distributed. The chief and the wealthy profited off the gold, and the rest of the villagers did not.

"It's not clear if the bandits were disgruntled villagers unhappy with the status quo or real bandits who heard of the new village riches. Regardless, they stormed the village and took over. They seemed to know who was wealthy and who was not, and they targeted the wealthy. After the attack was over, rumors were that the gold taken from the rich was distributed to the more needy citizens.

"The village chief somehow got wind of the attack. Or perhaps he just reacted faster than the other wealthy villagers. He was nowhere to be found when the bandits took over. They searched his home and couldn't find any hidden stash of valuables.

"Now, the chief's son, who was not particularly popular in the village, was one of the people who were being held by the bandits. When they realized they couldn't find either his father or his father's money, it occurred to them he might know something about where one or both of those things could be found.

"Somehow, the young man escaped from the bandits. He knew the area around the village well and took off into the countryside."

Sebastian stood for a second, gesturing for the peddler to continue, and went to throw another branch on the fire. As he threw the new wood on the fire, there was a burst of flame from the existing embers and a brief shower of sparks.

"If he had been anyone other than the chief's son, the bandits would probably have just let him go, but the chief had been the main profiteer from the mine, and they needed to find his gold. The bandits got hold of some dogs and gave them the young man's scent from his room in his father's house.

"The chief's son was holed up somewhere in the woods when he heard the baying of the hounds. His plan to hide from the bandits wasn't going to work with dogs tracking him, so he took off running through the forest.

"The sun was setting as he tried wading upstream in a narrow creek. It slowed the dogs down, but he could hear them as they figured it out and resumed the chase.

"Night fell, and by the light of a full moon, the young man entered a clearing in the forest. He had no more options and was about to collapse on the grass when he heard a voice.

"'Climb up, and you can hide behind me,' it said. The chief's son had no idea who was speaking initially until suddenly, he realized it was the moon. He climbed a tree near the moon, jumped over, and found a convenient hiding space behind the glowing orb.

"The young man was getting used to his hiding place when the dogs, followed closely by the bandits, entered the clearing. The dogs sniffed, especially around the base of the tree he had climbed, but the bandits couldn't see anyone in the tree by the full moon's light.

"The young man saw and heard everything from his vantage point. Imagine his glee when he overheard the bandits discussing how the dogs had lost the trail. They were ready to abandon the chase when he failed to contain it and let out a laugh.

"The bandits heard the laugh and knew he was there even though they couldn't see him. They set up camp for the night and kept a watch.

"The chief's son was able to stay awake and alert for a while, but the stillness and his exhaustion from the evening's events eventually got to him, and he fell asleep. Sleeping, he tumbled out of his hiding place and fell to the ground.

"The bandits collected him and returned to the village. They found his father and the gold with the information they got from him."

The peddler lowered his voice and then his gaze to show he was done.

"That's the end?" said Sebastian. Maybe it was old Widow Clark's best speaking, but he was indignant. "What's the moral? What's the point? Where's the happy ending?"

The peddler smiled. "Who says every story has to have a happy ending? Or a moral?

"Maybe it's just something which really happened," he said.

39

L ilith had a customer. She usually liked to put on a bit of a show. She pulled the hood of her cloak down over her eyes. It made her look more mysterious. She had something simmering in the large cauldron she kept over her fireplace. (It was only some water she had added a bit of coloring and some exotic smelling spices to, but it definitely added to the ambiance.)

"Well, my dear," she cackled. "What can I help you with today?"

The customer was young and female. Lilith estimated her age at about fourteen. Lilith recognized her by sight but not by name. The town was small enough so that it was hard not to know everyone, but she didn't spend too much time with the village children.

The girl seemed nervous. It must have been a struggle for her to muster the courage to ask for help. Lilith felt a touch of admiration for the effort.

The girl was still dressed in her school clothes. Mrs. Shoemaker had tried to enforce a school uniform, but it hadn't worked. She had, however, implemented a dress code.

The young customer looked around at the interior of Lilith's cottage. In addition to the cauldron, Lilith had some of her spices hanging from hooks on the ceiling. She had arranged rows of jars containing interesting-looking things on both sides of the fireplace. Most of the items were spices or just decorations, but some legitimate potion ingredients were among them.

Lilith's black cat Brinley stuck his head out from behind one of the jars. He hissed at the girl. She jumped and took a step backward. Lilith appreciated the gesture from Brinley, but she wished he had saved it for a more significant time. Impressing this girl was a little too easy.

Lilith decided this was enough. She stepped forward, reached out, and took the girl's hand. "Don't be scared, my dear," she said. "How can I help you?" Brinley saw the way things were going, jumped down off the shelf, walked over, and started rubbing against the girl's legs.

The girl hesitated a moment, then noticeably relaxed a little. She reached down and petted Brinley.

"I'm Constance," she said. "I … I heard you can make a love potion?"

This was not too different from what Lilith expected. More often than not, when a young person asked for help, it was something along these lines. Lilith had a standard disclaimer she gave.

"It's not really a love potion," she explained. "It's a potion which makes a person reconsider their attitude toward you. It gives you a new chance at a first impression. So is this boy you're interested in someone at school?"

"She's not a boy. Who said anything about a boy? She's beautiful, and she ignores me," said Constance.

Lilith was intrigued. At least a little different from the usual.

"The price is one copper coin and the memory of a summer day."

Lilith had no idea how to capture the memory of a summer day and even less of an idea what to do with it if she did. Adding something magical to the price gave her a certain mystique. It also made the customer think twice about whether or not they really needed their purchase.

Constance didn't hesitate. She produced the coin in a flash and waited for whatever magical extraction Lilith would need to do.

Lilith pocketed the coin and put on a little show of extracting the memory. She gave Constance the potion and a description of how to use it.

Constance thanked her and started to walk out the door.

"Constance," said Lilith, smiling, "come back and tell me how it went."

40

Sebastian dreamt he opened his eyes. He dreamt he sat up and looked around the campfire. The peddler wasn't there, but a glowing form sat across the fire from where Sebastian lay. Sebastian didn't recognize the figure, but he knew the glow. It was the same glow that came from his shield. It was the soft, gentle glow of a moonlit night.

The man in the moon, Sebastian thought. Though it was evident that she was a woman. *Of course she is*, he thought, though he couldn't remember why it had seemed so obvious when recalling the dream the next day.

She had her mouth open in the expressive "o" of shock he always saw when he gazed at the moon. Though it looked less like shock and more like mild outrage at this moment. Her expression changed to a friendly smile when she saw Sebastian looking at her.

"Sebastian," she said, "at last, we meet."

Sebastian didn't know how to respond. Several things struck him dumb about this. First off, this didn't feel like a dream to him. It felt more real than many waking moments he had had. Second, the moon was beautiful. She wore a flowing gown that glowed with the same soft moonlight which shone from her face, and that face was just stunning. He felt like he was in the presence of royalty, and although he didn't really know what that felt like, it was clear this was it.

"No reason to be alarmed about this," she said. "But I'm here to let you know you're being robbed."

Sebastian started and looked around himself. There was nothing to see except himself, the circle of firelight, and the moon.

"Don't worry," said the moon. "No time will pass in the

waking world while we talk. We have a moment.

"I just wanted to say," the moon continued, "I am enjoying this calling. They're not all pleasant, and it's nice to have one that feels worthwhile."

Sebastian made a conscious effort to make the expression on his face look a little less befuddled. He had no clue what was going on, but he didn't have to make that obvious.

"Be easy on him," she concluded. "He has his reasons."

41

Sebastian was using the saddlebag with the moon and Leonard's cap in it as his pillow. He woke up with the feeling that his pillow had moved. Sebastian sat bolt upright, with his hand flying immediately to the hilt of his sword. He wasn't sure where that reaction came from, but it served him well at this moment, as the peddler was only inches away from him with his hand on the laces of the saddlebag.

"Stop right now," Sebastian said.

The peddler stepped back, waving his hands, and tried to make some excuse.

"Don't even try," said Sebastian. "I know what you were doing." He looked over at his other saddlebags and saw they were all open. It seemed the peddler had looked through the easier ones before getting to the one under Sebastian's head.

Sebastian pulled the sword from its sheath. He meant to keep it ready, though he really didn't want to have a reason to use it.

"Did you take anything out of those bags?" he asked.

"No," said the peddler, looking sincerely ashamed. "I was looking for the moon. You don't have any idea what you have there."

"I know it's not mine to give away, sell or keep," said Sebastian. "And it's certainly not yours."

It was still the earliest stages of the dawn twilight.

"That thing," said the peddler, "would be worth a fortune to some people. I would have enough to buy a castle for my family.

"Times have been tough," he continued. "I had to sell my donkey to replenish my stock."

"You have a family?" said Sebastian.

"I haven't seen my family in almost a year. And I haven't had enough money to bring them anything for even longer."

"Pack up your stuff," Sebastian said. "I shouldn't do this, but I'll see if I can do something for you."

While the peddler got his belongings together, Sebastian plucked some grass blades and wove them into a grass ring. He kept an eye on the peddler as he did this to make sure he didn't get anywhere near the saddlebags.

Sebastian opened the saddlebag with the moon in it and took the little grass ring he had woven. He reached into the bag and touched the grass to the moon. There was a brief flash of light, then the woven grass started glowing with a shine that resembled the moon's glow. The weaving seemed to tighten and solidify.

Sebastian walked over to the peddler and handed him the ring. "Here," he said. "Take this. You can call it a moon ring. See if you can sell it. Now get going. I don't want to see you again."

The peddler looked curiously at the ring and took it eagerly.

"What does it do?" he said.

"How would I know?" said Sebastian.

"Can you make me another one?"

"Don't push it," said Sebastian. "Now, go!"

42

The mayor was in a private meeting. Mr. Arkwright, the smith, was one of the town aldermen. The town council comprised the mayor and the five prominent citizens who were the aldermen. Mr. Arkwright and the mayor were discussing critical town business. The mayor liked to think of all town business as critical.

"I've got four sketches of different proposed designs for the monument," said the mayor.

"The cobbles near where the beast fell seem to be permanently stained blue," said Mr. Arkwright.

"That's great," said the mayor. He rubbed his hands together as he spoke. "We'll put the monument right where it died."

"Where's the list of possible new names?" said Mr. Arkwright.

There was a knock on the door. The mayor sighed as he called out. "Come in." If this were a real town, no one would interrupt the middle of an important meeting.

The town hall didn't have a regular assistant, so different villagers volunteered to help. Anne, the miller's eldest daughter, was helping today.

"Mrs. Fletcher is here to see you, sir," she said. "She's very insistent."

The woman in question pushed past her through the doorway as she spoke. Mrs. Fletcher was the cobbler's wife. Also, Gerard's mother. Of course, being the cobbler's son was why Gerard always had the most elegant shoes in the village.

"Of course," said the mayor. "There is never a wrong moment to check in on the status of the merchants of our great metropolis."

"That's not what I'm here about," said Mrs. Fletcher, never one to bandy about an issue.

"Well then, my dear lady," said the mayor, "may I ask what you're here about?"

"It's Sebastian," she said. "When he comes back, you need to arrest him."

The mayor hesitated a moment before saying, "May I ask why?"

"He did something to my Gerard," she said. "He's always been such a strong boy. So sure of himself, so confident. Now, he won't hardly leave his room. He won't do anything. He says he's just waiting for Sebastian to come back."

"And you think Sebastian had something to do with this," said the mayor.

"When he took his shirt," said Mrs. Fletcher. "He took something else from him."

"Well, thank you, Mrs. Fletcher, for bringing this to my attention," said the mayor. "I assure you I will look into it." He realized as he spoke that there hadn't been any accounts of issues with Gerard in a while. In the past, he'd had to deal with a relatively steady stream of reports of someone feeling harassed, bar fights, or other altercations, and that had died down.

As Mrs. Fletcher thanked him and turned to leave, the mayor stepped back to his desk to look for the list of new town names for Mr. Arkwright.

43

Sebastian and Betsy were feeling aimless again. Sebastian was excited when he heard the peddler talk about a cave called the cave of nightmares in the foothills. That really seemed like something he should check out. So after scaring the peddler off in the morning, they tried to look for it. Unfortunately, there were no road signs which read, "Cave of Nightmares," and they didn't run into anyone to ask.

So far, they had been staying on the paths and trails. Sebastian worried that maybe the cave of nightmares was somewhere off the beaten path. If that were the case, they would never find it without some help.

They wandered around aimlessly for several hours. It was about noon, and the noonday sun blazed overhead. Sebastian dripped sweat and was not in a great mood.

He turned to Betsy and said, "Why do I have to be in charge. Why can't you take care of things for a while?"

He loosened his hold on the lead and gave her a look. She stared right back at him and, sensing the slackness on the strap, took off down a grassy bank on one side of the road. Sebastian hadn't expected this effort to succeed and was a little startled. She was moving quickly, and he struggled to keep up with her.

"Betsy," he called out. "Wait for me!" Sebastian hoped whatever spirit was guiding him, and this expedition had taken hold of Betsy. Maybe she would lead them to the cave.

She seemed to know where she was going. Sebastian followed her for what felt like a long time but probably wasn't more than a few minutes. Sebastian heard a splashing sound as they pushed through some thicker underbrush. He put his hand on the hilt of his sword. Maybe they were getting close to the cave.

As they cleared the brush, he saw a babbling stream

ahead. There was a green meadow between him, Betsy, and the creek. Betsy was making a beeline for the water. Sebastian gave up. The green field and the flowing water looked fresh and inviting. He let Betsy drink a bit, removed her saddlebags, and settled her down to graze. He lay down for a nap in the shade of a weeping willow whose branches trailed into the stream's water. He plunked his head down on a saddlebag and was sound asleep in no time.

44

Sebastian dreamt again that he opened his eyes. He dreamt again that he sat up. The glow of the full moon was shining around him. He looked around and wasn't surprised to see the woman in the moon sitting cross-legged on the grass a little ways away from him. It did surprise him to see Betsy standing between where he was and the stream. Betsy nickered with gratitude. She was pleased to be part of the dream this time.

Even sitting cross-legged on the ground, the moon lady was more elegant and graceful than anything Sebastian had ever seen. He really had no idea how to speak to her. She reached somewhere in her glowing robe and pulled out a carrot that she held out in Betsy's direction. Surprising Sebastian, as he'd never seen Betsy hesitate to do anything, except listen to him, Betsy inched hesitantly over to the lady. The mule reached out, pulling her lips back from her teeth, and gently pulled the carrot out of the moon lady's hand.

Raising her voice a little to be heard over the crunching carrot sounds, the woman said, "Sebastian, you seemed a little lost today."

Sebastian felt this needed a response, so he mustered his courage and asked, "Have you been watching me?"

"It's a little hard to see much from inside your saddlebags, but I have my ways," she replied.

"Yes, we are lost," Sebastian said. "I'm not even sure I know how to get back to the road from here. Miss... What should I call you?"

"Call me, Luna," said the woman with a smile.

"Miss Luna," said Sebastian.

"Just Luna," she said.

"That feels a little informal," Sebastian said sheepishly.

Luna laughed. The sound was like the babble of a moonlit stream running over mossy rocks at midnight on a beautiful clear summer night. Betsy stopped crunching her carrot for a moment and looked over at her. Then she snapped up the last bite and started sniffing at Luna's robes for more.

Luna produced another carrot from somewhere and spoke again. "I think I can help."

"We will appreciate whatever you can do," said Sebastian. "We're really lost."

"It should be evening twilight when you wake," Luna said. "Look for help in the twilight. I'll send someone to help you."

45

William knocked. The door muffled the sound, but he thought he heard someone call out. He opened the door and stepped inside. It felt a little stuffy. William thought maybe he should try to get some air flowing.

"Reynard?" he said.

"Back here," came the reply from a back room. "They're not letting me get up, or I'd answer the door."

There were various foodstuffs and other supplies on the table in the front room. William added the bread and the other food he was carrying to the rest.

He headed back into Reynard's bedroom.

"You hungry?" he said.

"Hi, William," said Reynard. "I was wondering when you'd get around to visiting."

William flushed, then he saw that Reynard had a big smile on his face.

"Oh, well," he said, "I figured you had enough visitors with the whole town looking in on you."

William inspected Reynard and was genuinely embarrassed. Reynard looked terrible. One side of his face was still bruised and scraped up. One leg and one of his arms were in splints. He should have checked in sooner.

"None of them will play cards with me," said Reynard.

"Well, it's a good thing I'm here then," said William, and he pulled a deck of cards out of a pocket.

46

When Sebastian woke, he noticed a small puddle of drool on the side of the saddlebag he was using as a pillow. He flushed and hoped Luna hadn't somehow seen him drooling. Betsy leaned her head over him and started pushing up against him. He realized Betsy must have seen him drooling, but that didn't bother him as much. He also thought the way Betsy was pushing her head against him was very reminiscent of how she had sniffed at Luna's robes in his dream.

"I don't have any carrots," he said.

The sun was setting. Sebastian looked around to see any sign of the help Luna had promised. There was no one there but him and Betsy. He got up and reloaded the mule. The night shadows were getting thicker, but he hoped his dream would help him find his way, and he didn't want to miss the promised help.

Betsy and Sebastian started off toward the mountains. They didn't really know which way to go, but Sebastian concluded that caves would be more likely in the foothills.

They walked for quite a while without seeing anyone. Sebastian even called out at one point, though he felt foolish as he didn't know who he was calling out to. The oncoming darkness made it hard to keep going. Sebastian had an idea. The idea had occurred to him earlier, but he hadn't wanted to try it on the main road.

He held Betsy's lead to stop her so he could open the saddlebag containing the moon. His idea was to wear the moon on his arm and travel by its light. The full moon's light was usually enough to allow one to see pretty well at night. Even though nights were dark since Sebastian liberated the moon from the sky, the night didn't have to be dark for him.

As soon as he opened the saddlebag, a brilliant light beam shot out into the darkening twilight sky. The glow seemed to twirl around in a descending spiral. Something about how the little ray of light shot out of the saddlebag, through the night sky, and back toward Sebastian and Betsy made it look joyful. As if it was glad to be free of the saddlebag.

The beam of moonlight formed into a ball and danced in the air in front of Sebastian's face. It bopped up and down as if nodding. Sebastian had let go of the open flap of the saddlebag when the light shot out. The flap closed, but the glow didn't go out.

"Hi," came a voice. It was gleeful, high-pitched, and sounded distant like it was a voice and the echo of the same voice simultaneously.

"Hi," said Sebastian carefully.

"I thought you'd never find me," said the voice. "Luna sent me to help. I'm Moonbeam."

47

Moonbeam chirped, "This'll be so much fun. I haven't spent a whole night down here in a really long time." The light ray bopped up and down excitedly, though it slowed toward the last word.

"I'll have to leave in the morning," it finished sadly.

Sebastian watched, trying to see how the voice came out of the bouncing ball of light. The light pulsed and bounced up and down with the rhythm of the words. That was about all he could make out. There was a shower of motes of brightness whenever the voice finished speaking and the feeling of an echo.

"We're not too tired," Sebastian said. "I had a good nap under the willow tree, but I'm not sure we can walk all night."

"Follow me!" said Moonbeam, and he, she, or maybe it, zoomed gleefully up the hill. Moonbeam was zipping back and forth over the hillside and glowing almost as brightly as a full moon.

"Hey, Moonbeam," Sebastian called out hesitantly. "Maybe you could slow down a little? Also, maybe we should turn down the light show a bit?"

Insomuch as a floating ball of light can look embarrassed, Moonbeam did. "Sorry," it said. "I got excited."

The glow seemed to dim a bit.

Moonbeam floated over to Betsy. It drifted around her head. Betsy cocked one ear forward and the other back as she snapped her teeth at the floating ball of light.

Moonbeam zipped hurriedly out of the way of Betsy's teeth. Its light dimmed and then brightened again as it spun in a spiral around the mule's head. Betsy swung her head around to follow the glow, then gave up. Moonbeam continued up the hill more slowly.

"Why do you have to leave in the morning?" asked Sebastian as he pulled Betsy's lead up the hill.

Moonbeam flitted over to hover in front of Sebastian's face. Somehow he got the impression he had said something ridiculous. "Moon spirits aren't much good during the day," said Moonbeam. "No one can see or hear us."

They reached the top of the ridge, and Moonbeam led them on confidently. It seemed to be leading them further into the hills. The pleasant moon glow it cast over the way was enough to see where they were going.

"How do you know which way to go?" said Sebastian. "Is there a trail leading to the cave, or do we have to cut cross-country?"

"You wouldn't believe the view from up there," somehow Moonbeam indicated the sky as it said this. "You want a trail? Isn't that dumb? Why don't you just fly, like me?"

There was a moment of silence as Moonbeam considered what it had just said.

"Sorry," it said. "I forgot."

The direction Moonbeam was leading them seemed to change a little, and Sebastian hoped this showed it was trying to find a trail for them to follow.

Sebastian noticed Betsy's ears plaster back on her head a half-second before hearing what she heard. It was a howling sound, the call of a wolf. It was too close for comfort. Sebastian's hand went instinctively to the hilt of his sword.

Moonbeam noticed them stopping and started bopping up and down like a firefly.

"I'll go see," it said.

The beam of moonlight shot straight up into the air and raced off toward the sound. Moonbeam's absence left Sebastian and Betsy in almost complete darkness. Sebastian thought about opening his saddlebag to let a little light out, but he decided to wait. Betsy was quivering on the lead. He felt around in the darkness until he found her side and stroked her to calm her.

Moonbeam returned just as quickly as it had left. It

dropped to the level it was at before and bopped up and down again.

"It's all right. The wolves are going the other way," Moonbeam said.

Moonbeam led them on through the night. After a little while, they pushed through some brush onto a narrow meandering trail.

As they walked along the trail, the lunar spirit commented, "plod, plod, plod."

It seemed to enjoy the sound it had made and started singing a little song.

"Plod, plod, over the sod. Trudge, trudge, through the sludge.

"Clump, clump, around the stump. Tramp, tramp, to the camp."

Moonbeam sang the same song for what felt like hours. It started becoming less enjoyable for Sebastian. Eventually, even Moonbeam seemed to tire of it, and it stopped. They trudged on in silence for a while.

As the first glimmer of dawn showed in the morning sky, Sebastian realized how tired he was. They had walked through the night. Betsy showed signs of exhaustion as well. Her head was down, and her nostrils were flaring. Sebastian expected laid-back ears and a refusal to continue at some point.

Moonbeam stopped and indicated the trail ahead. "You're almost there. I did good, didn't I? The cave is just a little further on."

"Are you sure you have to leave us?" said Sebastian. He'd only just met Moonbeam, but he was sad about this. It'd been nice to have someone take charge, and Moonbeam was so cheerful.

"Gotta go," said Moonbeam. "But just remember, once we're back up in the sky, you'll see me every night!"

Moonbeam drifted over to Betsy. The flap to her saddlebag flew open, seemingly by itself. With a flash of light, or perhaps *as* a flash of light, Moonbeam disappeared into the bag. The flap dropped closed, and then the only light was the morning twilight and the twinkling stars.

Sebastian found a spot he didn't think was visible from the trail and set up his tent. He took off Betsy's saddlebags and tied her in a place where she could graze. Then he crawled into his tent and fell sound asleep.

48

The mayor banged his gavel hard enough to make at least one tired alderman start. "This meeting of the Westhavenfieldbrook city council will come to order." As much as the word town always gave the mayor a little pleasure, the word city sent an electric shock of joy through his body.

The mayor and the five aldermen sat in the town hall meeting room. Rows of chairs were facing them, but only one villager was present. It was Mrs. Fletcher. The mayor was reasonably sure she was here to raise the idea of arresting Sebastian. He hoped to put off talking to her as long as possible.

The mayor banged his gavel again. This time everyone started. He wasn't sure what the protocol was on when he was and wasn't supposed to use it, but it seemed to get everyone's attention, and he enjoyed doing it.

"If I could have your attention, please," he said. "This portion of the meeting is a closed session. If I could have the bailiff clear the room, please."

There was no bailiff. Today, Anne, the miller's eldest daughter, was the town hall volunteer. She looked a little surprised, but she stepped forward. She walked over to Mrs. Fletcher and held out her hand to help her stand.

After Mrs. Fletcher had left the room, the mayor continued, "If we could have the secretary read the minutes from the last meeting," he said.

Anne stood again, lifted a paper, and read a detailed description of what happened in the last meeting. They had discussed funding a monument to commemorate the recent battle between Sebastian and the beast. They had also discussed ways to make the village of Westhavenfieldbrook attractive to tourists.

"New business," said Mr. Arkwright. "As you all know, we've been talking about a new name for the village. Westhavenfieldbrook is descriptive, but it's at the very least a mouthful."

There were some muttered responses from the other aldermen. It seemed this idea had some fans and some opponents.

"Our esteemed mayor," continued Mr. Arkwright. The mayor preened a little when he heard himself mentioned. "Has come up with a proposed name which has some potential advantages. Let's give him our attention."

"We'd have to redo the road signs," one alderman muttered.

"It's been the name of the village since before I was born," another one said.

The mayor began, "the issue we have had in times past with the discussion of a possible new town name has been that we couldn't agree on a name. You all know about my plans to see if we can get a bit of a tourist industry going in our town. In light of that effort, I propose we rename Westhavenfieldbrook to Hero. Welcome to the town of Hero!"

49

It was twilight again when Sebastian awoke. At first, he wasn't sure if morning or evening twilight was lighting the canvas walls of his tent, but he felt rested, so he quickly realized he had slept the day away.

He stepped out of the tent into the last rays of a fading sunset. Betsy was contentedly cropping grass not far away. It was a very peaceful moment, and Sebastian hated to leave it, but he had things to do. He opened the saddlebag containing the moon and brought out both the moon and Leonard's cap. When Sebastian lifted the moon out of the bag, it seemed like a piece of light shining from the moon isolated itself and spiraled gracefully around his hand.

As he adjusted his armor, including checking his mending of the rip in Gerard's shirt, he felt a momentary flash of pride. "The Knight of Moon and Shadow" was not such a bad thing to be called. He could also be called "The Bearer of the Gifts." Though he thought the first one had more of a ring to it.

Sebastian hung Leonard's cap through his belt. In case he needed some foolishness or some foolhardiness. He put his forearm through the straps behind the moon and checked to make sure his sword was loose and free in its sheath.

Moonbeam had said the cave was nearby, so Sebastian left the tent set up. Betsy was contentedly grazing and looked very comfortable, so Sebastian thought she would be fine. He loosened the lead. Not enough so she could leave immediately, but just enough so if he didn't come back, she should be able to free herself with a bit of effort.

He scratched her between the ears, in the spot where he thought she liked it. She nickered and licked his face. She put one ear back and the other forward in the way he read as inquisitive.

"I'll be back soon," he said. "Unless I'm not."

Sebastian stepped over onto the path. He followed it a little further. As Moonbeam had said, it wasn't far to the cave. Around the next bend, the trail led into a clearing.

On the far side of the clearing was a rock face with an ancient opening. A jagged crack in the rock opened broadly enough at the bottom that two people could walk in side by side. The cave was clearly lived in, as the trail led right into the crevice.

The clearing was lit by starlight, the last trace of fading light from the setting sun, and the moonlight from Sebastian's shield.

Sebastian immediately knew he was in the right place. Standing in the middle of the clearing was another nightmare, twin to the one that had attacked the village.

50

Sebastian took a second to assess the situation. Either the beast hadn't detected him yet, or perhaps it just wasn't feeling challenged. It seemed to be ignoring him for the moment. On the other hand, there was probably not going to be any way around it. The path led, both figuratively and literally, right through the nightmare.

It looked the same as the other beast he had fought, in one way. In another, it seemed entirely different. When he faced the monster back in the village, there had been a crowd of people there. The creature took on something of the fears and dreams of the people watching. Now, it was just the beast and Sebastian.

Sebastian stepped into the clearing. Immediately the creature turned in his direction. A rushing sound like rocks scraping together as they rolled down a hill filled the air as the beast charged toward him. Sebastian lifted his shield and drew his sword.

He thought about pulling Leonard's cap from his belt, but he felt sufficiently in control of this situation. It wasn't time to look for Leonard's help yet. Sebastian held the shield between himself and the beast to deflect whatever blow it would throw. Then he sidestepped the attack using the speed he felt flowing into his legs from Pico's pants.

The beast roared as it rushed past Sebastian and its tentacle clanged off the moon. It was close enough that the wind of its passing surrounded him. His sense of smell felt heightened. Perhaps something to do with Pico's gift. He smelled the beast. It smelled of moss and mold. It smelled of the mushrooms you might find growing in a crevice at the base of an old oak tree in the middle of a shadowy forest.

Sebastian felt like laughing. He felt full of daring. He

knew how to fight this beast. It was old news. He wouldn't need Leonard's cap, but he knew where his confidence came from. He had the gifts. He had support. He had Isabel, Luna, Moonbeam, Pico, Leonard, his father, and even Gerard helping him.

From there, the battle was mainly rote. Sebastian felt for the creature. He was faster than it with the pants of the wind. He could fade into the shadows if he needed to. Gerard's shirt was giving him confidence. He could deflect the creature's blows with the moon. It was almost unfair.

There were a series of feints and parries like the battle in the village, but the conclusion seemed preordained. Sebastian tried to think of some way he could spare the beast from the coup de grâce. But as far as he could tell, the creature was mainly mindless and wouldn't stop until he killed it.

As he delivered the final blow, Sebastian felt sorry for the creature. It disappeared, like the one in the village had, leaving the stones and earth of the clearing stained with the same blue that covered some of the village square cobblestones.

Sebastian walked over to the cave entrance and entered the cave of nightmares.

51

The cavern led back into the mountain. Soon after passing the rough rock of the cave mouth, the walls looked smoother. Someone had worked the walls of this cavern into a smooth tunnel at some point. The moon glow from Sebastian's shield, and the light from a series of glowing stones about eye height on the cave walls, broke the tunnel's darkness. The glow from the rocks was a sickly blue color, but the warm moonlight from Sebastian's arm overpowered it.

The air in the tunnel was damp and smelled a little moldy. Sebastian heard nothing. He tried to keep quiet to not announce his presence, though the battle outside with the nightmare might have already spoiled that effort.

The walls of the tunnel opened outward as it widened into a chamber. Sebastian thought the space was empty for a second, then he shivered as he saw what was filling the cavern. It was packed from top to bottom with webs. Not spider webs; these webs were the weaving of tent caterpillars. Sebastian heard a rustling sound like thousands of tiny legs scurrying over webbing.

Sebastian's memory flashed back to one summer when, as a child, he had been climbing a tree on a quiet summer evening while his father tended to the cows. He was high in the tree, disregarding his father's warnings. As he reached the top of the tree and raised his head to see the view, he lost his footing.

Sebastian didn't remember the details of the fall, except for the sensation of falling, which he never forgot. But he remembered the landing. He didn't make it to the ground. There was a stunning impact, which knocked the wind out of him, and he lost consciousness for a moment.

He had landed flat on a broad branch, with his arms and

legs straddling both sides of the limb, somehow balanced, so he didn't fall further. The part that stuck in his memory and nightmares was how he landed with his face right inside a tent caterpillar's nest.

Sebastian had recovered awareness with the caterpillars climbing over his face and with one in his mouth. He couldn't see anything except the insects and the white of the silk tent. He tried to call out for help, but the insect in his mouth and the silk around his head muffled his cries.

Since that day, Sebastian's idea of hell was slightly different from most people's. What he saw in this cave was that hell.

He stood in the tunnel mouth. The scuttling noise he had heard earlier was growing more intense. Sebastian was convinced he could see shapes moving in the silken tent webbing. Whatever was scuttling about there was long and thin and bigger than any insect had a right to be.

Sebastian thought about drawing his sword and trying to cut through the webs, but he couldn't even start to move his hand. He took a step backward. He shook his head. This really wasn't going to work.

It occurred to him that a change of perspective might help. He pulled Leonard's cap out of his belt. Sebastian hesitated. His worry about putting Leonard's gift on his head was whether he would ever be in the frame of mind to remove it again.

Sebastian slapped the cap on his head. Immediately things did feel different. It wasn't that he wasn't afraid anymore. Or that he disregarded the fear. It was more like his priorities had changed.

The quest was unimportant. The fear was insignificant. What interested Sebastian now was the notion of a caterpillar more than a foot long.

Sebastian stepped forward. Reaching out toward the nearest web, he looked for one where there seemed to be something moving behind it. He tried to grab the webbing to pull it aside like a curtain. His hand went through the web as if it wasn't there.

He stuck his head through the web. He felt nothing. He could still hear the scuttling sound and see the webbing. He could even smell something like his memory of the tent and the caterpillars from his fall. But when he tried to touch it, there was nothing there.

Sebastian was confused; perhaps the word baffled might apply. He stood there partway through the tent wall, having trouble figuring out what was going on. He reached up to his head and pulled Leonard's cap back off.

Sebastian blinked. Things seemed clearer. He remembered Lorenzo's description of the discipline of illusion. He tucked the cap back into his belt. Lorenzo had described an illusion as a spell that fooled your senses, specifically vision, hearing, and smell, but wasn't physically there. Sebastian waved his hand through the web again. He felt nothing.

He knew what he had to do. He had to walk through the chamber, ignoring the visions, sounds, and smells, until he got to the other side.

Sebastian drew his sword and tapped it like the cane of a blind man to find his way across the cavern. The sights and sounds still brought back bad memories but knowing they were not solid helped.

He made it across the chamber and found a tunnel continuing further into the earth on the other side.

52

I sabel was delivering some chairs for her mother. She led a cart loaded with five chairs down Main Street toward the market square. The chairs were being taken to the town hall. One was the original, which her mother had needed to create perfect copies, and the other four were those copies. Her mother had spent more than an hour on just the color of the stain. She made sure the shade was precisely right, so you couldn't tell the copies from the original.

The mayor had ordered the chairs for the meeting hall. He expected town hall meetings to have more attendees in the future, and the chairs were one small step to prepare for that. He assured Mrs. Fisher there would be more orders coming.

Anise was helping with the delivery. At the moment, her help was slightly less than helpful. She had an apple and walked next to George, the draft horse, who was supposed to be busy pulling the cart.

Isabel sometimes thought of George as "George, the dragon slayer." Not because he had slain any dragons, but because he had a mighty kick. He had broken down his stall door at least once, forcing Mrs. Fisher to make a new, stronger one. Isabel imagined if a dragon were ever to stand behind George, the dragon slayer part of his name might come true.

Anise's apple kept causing George to pull to the side, so Isabel had to keep pulling the opposite way on the reins to keep the cart straight.

"Just give him the apple, Anise," said Isabel.

Anise did so, and soon the sound of contented crunching filled the air.

"Are you and Sebastian going to get married?" said Anise.

"What?" Isabel flushed.

"Are you going to get married?"

"Why would you ask that?" Isabel's flush got a bit deeper.

"Well," said Anise. "You kissed him when he left on his quest."

"Anise," said Isabel. "I kissed him on the cheek. It was to thank him for saving the village. Anyway, one kiss doesn't mean you have to get married."

"It doesn't?" said Anise.

"No. It doesn't."

"Oh," said Anise. She paused thoughtfully for a moment before continuing. "Well, I wouldn't mind if you got married. I might even like it."

Isabel smiled. "Well, thank you for your blessing, Anise," she said.

53

Sebastian stepped into a larger open chamber. It was still carved from the rock, but this chamber was set up as a living area. Tapestries warmed the rock walls, and carpets covered the stone floor.

A man stood in the center of the room. He wore a worn robe, the sort you might see at an educational institution or on a monk. It was threadbare, nearly in tatters, but it might once have been made of exquisite material. In some ways, the man looked as worn as his robe. He was old, by Sebastian's standards, ancient. He looked alert, however, and perhaps dangerous.

Sebastian's mouth dropped open in shock. He hadn't recognized him, at first, as he was dressed differently and looked older. But his face was the same, and it was impossible to fail to acknowledge his mustache. It was Lorenzo.

"Enzo?" Sebastian said. "What are you doing here?"

"Trying to get rid of you," said Lorenzo, with a trace of the same smile he had worn as they sat by the campfire. As he spoke, he made a curious gesture with his hands. He held them together, all ten fingers spread out, and made a pushing motion toward Sebastian with his arms.

A small darting flame shot out from the tip of each finger. The ten little darting bolts of fire all homed in on Sebastian. He stepped back and raised the moon between himself and the fiery darts. They splattered against the moon, one by one, with Sebastian being knocked back another half step as each one broke on the shield.

Sebastian lowered his shield and stepped forward. Lorenzo's face drew his attention. It was the same face he had grown to like as they had shared a meal a few days ago, but today the expression was harsher. There was cruelty showing there that

Sebastian hadn't seen before. As he studied Lorenzo's face, Sebastian was careful to avoid looking at the whorls of his mustache. Probably that was more dangerous than Lorenzo had told him as well.

"I don't understand. How did I meet you on the road if you've been here?" Sebastian asked.

"I had to see what I was facing," said Lorenzo, and Sebastian recognized the signs of him starting to cast a spell. This time Lorenzo held both hands together and swept them from left to right across the open space in front of himself. A mighty wind started, blowing from Sebastian's right. It was fiercer than any wind Sebastian had felt before, and it would have swept him aside if it hadn't been for his trousers. Where the wind touched the white material of his pants, it seemed to blow through the fabric without any pressure. With the wind not affecting his legs, Sebastian could resist the tempest and continue to move forward.

Lorenzo took a step backward when that attempt to slow Sebastian failed. He seemed like he was considering what to try next.

Sebastian stopped moving for a second. He had a moment of grief, like someone he knew had died.

"Lorenzo," he couldn't bring himself to use the nickname Enzo, as it felt like that was the name of a person who was gone. "So, everything you said to me was a lie?"

"Not really," said Lorenzo, "a lot of that is who I used to be." He made another gesture, with one hand this time, a cupping gesture, and a globe of water rose from a tub on the other side of the room. Lorenzo swept the cupped hand in Sebastian's direction, releasing the fingers as he did so. The ball of water swept toward Sebastian, moving at an incredible speed. But Sebastian was already gone when the liquid broke over where he had been. He used the Boots of Shadow to step into the darkness and reappear in another place in the room.

Lorenzo sighed wearily. He rubbed his hand over his eyes.

"Well, this isn't getting us anywhere," he said. "Perhaps

we should sit down and talk. Would you like a cup of tea?"

54

S ebastian warily made his way over to the table and chairs that Lorenzo pointed out to him. He sat and waited a moment while Lorenzo bustled about making some tea. The contrast with what had just been happening was disturbing for him. He tried to calm his breath and let his adrenaline settle.

"What did you mean when you said that was what you used to be?" he called out to Lorenzo.

Lorenzo walked over to the table with a loaded tea tray.

"The man you met on the road is pretty much who I used to be, years ago, before I went to that damn academy I told you about. I learned many things there, some of which I'd be happier not knowing."

He put the tray on the table and put cups in front of Sebastian and himself.

"I used to travel around in that cart, giving shows and selling services, exactly like I told you. I haven't used it in years. It was nostalgic to dig it out and go on the road with it, if only for a while."

Sebastian remembered something he should have noticed at the time. The corners of the cart and some of the supplies were dusty and cobwebbed. He should have known something was up. He'd just thought of it as poor housekeeping.

Sebastian rested the moon beside him as he sat, leaning her against his leg. He wanted to have her near to hand, just in case.

Lorenzo continued. "Then, I got the idea that I wanted to learn. I wasn't actually as hostile to the academy as I made it sound. Anyway, I enrolled. One thing I told you, which was a lie, was about me and channeling. Channeling was actually my strength." Lorenzo looked proud for a moment. "In fact, they didn't know what to do with me, as I was a stronger channeler than most of my teachers."

Lorenzo paused for a moment and took a sip of his tea. He gestured towards Sebastian's cup with his chin, encouraging him to try it.

"Try the tea," he said. "I make it myself from local herbs."

Sebastian reached for his teacup. A mote of light from the moon shone out and flitted over by his hand. The slender light beam spiraled around his forearm as it moved toward the tea. The glowing mote blocked him from touching the cup. He pulled the hand back and dropped it to his side. The light faded back into the shield.

Lorenzo watched the ray of light block Sebastian from drinking the tea. He looked interested and disappointed at the same time. "You have a lot of friends helping you." He smiled. Again, Sebastian saw a hint of the smile he remembered from before.

"So what was it you said about learning things you would be happier not knowing?" said Sebastian. "And what does all this have to do with why you're attacking villages?"

"Those are both essentially the same question," said Lorenzo.

Sebastian had his right hand on his sword hilt. He wore both the locket with his mother's picture and her heart-shaped jade medallion around his neck. While Lorenzo was talking, he played with them with his left hand.

"That's nice," said Lorenzo, referring to the jade heart.

"It was my mother's," said Sebastian.

55

Old Widow Clark was talking to Mr. Thatcher, the farrier, in a stable attached to the side of his house. It was his place of business. The town didn't have a veterinarian. If you had a problem with an animal, you would either ask Mr. Thatcher if there was anything he could do, or you would talk to Lilith.

"My Pico," said old Widow Clark. "He won't bark anymore. He's so quiet and sad. I swear I don't know what to do."

Mr. Thatcher wondered why he was thinking of Mrs. Clark as old Widow Clark when she wasn't actually any older than he was. It just seemed that was what people were calling her nowadays.

"I'm sorry, Mrs. Clark," he said, "I don't know much about dogs. Wasn't it something Sebastian did to him? That's what I've heard people saying."

"I don't know anything about that," said Mrs. Clark firmly. "Maybe you need to express his anal gland?"

"I'm sure I don't need to do any such thing," said Mr. Thatcher, even more firmly.

56

L orenzo continued, "I studied at the academy. Graduated. In fact, a few years after graduating, I went back and became a teacher. I taught channeling. I was good at it. Teaching, I mean. I think I helped the students.

"The infighting among the staff got to me. I told you a little about that the last time we talked. I didn't tell you how bad it was. The teachers and administrators all had their domains. They would fight over the stupidest things.

"As I told you, one thing they fought over was which were true disciplines. But often, their reasons for arguing one way or another were about power or position at the academy, not whether it would help the students. Anyway, I had a student, a young woman, who was a good student but wasn't a channeler, an illusionist, an alchemist, or an elemental mage. Instead, she was a clairvoyant. I tried to argue that to help her, we should adopt the study of clairvoyance as a discipline, but no one would have anything to do with that. It would weaken their authority too much.

"She was haunted by what she saw of the future, by what she knew. No one would help her. No one could. I tried; I left the academy; I took her with me. I did my best to help her deal with her demons. I failed. I failed her. To this day, the fact that I couldn't help her torments me."

Sebastian interrupted. "I'm still not seeing how this connects to the nightmares."

"I'm getting there," said Lorenzo, "kids nowadays. No patience.

"I was recording her prophecies. Her predictions," Lorenzo continued. "There is no record of what she knew, what she saw, except what I wrote down.

"I retired here to study what she had known. A lot of it came true. Some important things, some more minor. Even the things that didn't come true left you feeling you knew why they hadn't.

"I guess I lost touch with the world a little. I've been camped out in this cave for years. I've been trying to help in my own way.

"Her most significant prediction was that a channeler would be born. More potent than any there had ever been before.

"I've seen the signs. This channeler has been born. The prophecies predicted this powerful channeler would fracture the world. Would disrupt things beyond belief; would cause reality to shatter into pieces. I have to eliminate the source before that can happen. Based on my reading of the signs, this channeler should still be a child, so I am trying to get rid of them before they can develop their powers.

"Channeling is the most powerful of the disciplines. It's also the hardest to control. An out of control or evil channeler can do enormous damage."

"Like you've done with your nightmares," said Sebastian.

"It's hard to target channeling," said Lorenzo, "I'm sorry about the collateral damage, but the ends justify the means."

"Collateral damage!" said Sebastian. "These are people's lives we're talking about!"

"I was trying for a surgical strike," said Lorenzo. "The nightmares were just supposed to kill the channeler."

"Surgical strike!" said Sebastian, "Anesbury was leveled. My village would have been as well!"

"That's why I sent the caretakers in," said Lorenzo. "I hoped they would help fix things up."

"All they did was bury the dead," said Sebastian.

57

Lorenzo got angry. It was the first time Sebastian saw him show any emotion other than amusement. "You stupid boy," he shouted, "why didn't you do what the peddler suggested. Just take your things, move somewhere, sell them, and settle down to a rich life."

"I couldn't," said Sebastian.

"I know," said Lorenzo sadly.

Lorenzo made another quick gesture. This time he clenched each hand into a fist and made a pulling motion like pulling two things toward himself.

Sebastian heard Luna's voice in his head.

"Sebastian," she said. "Behind you, quickly."

Sebastian grabbed the moon from beside his leg. It leapt into his hand. He whirled around and held up the shield. There were two loud thuds as two rock spikes crashed into the moon. Sebastian was forced back a step, but the protection held.

"Sebastian," said Lorenzo, "I had to do it. You don't know what this channeler will be capable of. Can you blame me?"

"Yes," said Sebastian. He spun quickly to face Lorenzo, raced over to him, and reached out to grab his hands. He thought that keeping Lorenzo's hands still might prevent him from casting a spell.

Lorenzo had looked vigorous when they sat at the campfire, but he must have been using illusions to hide his age. Sebastian found himself able to contain the older man.

Sebastian felt he had a dilemma. In some sense, the correct thing to do might be to kill Lorenzo. It could be the only way to stop him, and perhaps it was deserved for the damage he had done and the people he had killed.

But Sebastian couldn't bring himself to do it. For one

thing, the idea of the cold-blooded killing of a helpless person wasn't something he could conceive. For another, he still had some sympathy for Lorenzo and his story.

He had an inspiration. Holding Lorenzo's wrists in his right hand, he pulled the jade heart off his neck with his other hand. As the stone pulled away from Sebastian's chest, a small gray shadow moved with it. Sebastian lifted the necklace up and brought it toward Lorenzo. Lorenzo's eyes opened wide as he saw what was coming, and he struggled to get free of Sebastian's grip. But the younger man was stronger, and he dropped the necklace over Lorenzo's head.

As the jade pendant settled onto his chest, Lorenzo dropped to his knees and began to cry. Sebastian let go of the grip he had on Lorenzo's wrists.

Sebastian stepped over to Lorenzo. Lorenzo didn't seem to see him, as he was too involved in his grief. Sebastian reached out his index finger, placed it on the jade heart on Lorenzo's chest, and gently pushed. Nothing happened at first, then Sebastian felt another presence. Luna was with him, and he could feel the pressure of her invisible finger on top of his. His finger pressed into the jade heart and then through it. The force of his and Luna's fingers pushed the shadow out of the jade heart and into Lorenzo's chest.

58

Anise and Rose were having breakfast. Shining past the flowered curtains on the windows, sunshine spread across the kitchen table. With a bit of help from Anise, Rose had been baking all morning. The baked goods covered the counter. The delicious aroma of warm bread filled the kitchen.

"Isn't it a beautiful day, Aunt Rose?" said Anise.

"It is, Anise," said Rose, "You're in a good mood today."

"I'm happy," said Anise. "Sebastian is coming home soon. And Isabel's going to marry him."

"Is she, now," said Rose with a smile. She put some fresh pastries from the day's baking onto a plate in front of Anise.

"Now, Anise," said Rose, "Don't get too excited about Sebastian coming home soon. As far as I know, we haven't heard anything from him since he left. There's no way for him to let us know what he's up to."

Anise took a bite from the pastry in front of her. "He is coming home. I dreamed it last night."

"Anise," said Rose, "you know we talked about this. Dreams aren't real."

"I know yours aren't, Aunt Rose, but mine are. In my dream, Sebastian had a fight with the bad man."

Anise continued. "He beat him, Aunt Rose. He beat him, and he gave him a piece of his heart. The bad man's not a bad man anymore."

59

Sebastian and Betsy were camping just outside Anesbury again. Sebastian had set up the tent, and Betsy contentedly grazed near where Sebastian was starting a fire. They'd traveled for two days since leaving Lorenzo's cave. It relieved Sebastian to think they were halfway home.

Lorenzo hadn't taken well to his change of heart. He wept for ten minutes, then got furiously angry for another ten. When he switched from being sad to being angry, Sebastian kept a careful eye on him to see if he did anything dangerous. Especially for the start of a spell.

It was hard to get a coherent word out of Lorenzo while he was so angry. Still, it seemed like he was raging about how the academy hadn't listened to him when he tried to get them to accept the prophecies.

After his raging, Lorenzo became confused. Almost befuddled. Sebastian thought maybe he was trying to reconcile his thoughts with his new heart.

In the end, Lorenzo calmed down. When Sebastian could finally talk to him, he found a calm, quieter man struggling with regret for some of what he had done, but not all of it. Lorenzo still felt the prophecies' predictions were vital, but he regretted the violence of his methods.

Lorenzo found something in the prophecies that made him believe the new channeler would eventually make their way to the academy. He decided his best course forward was to help the academy prepare for this arrival.

Sebastian helped Lorenzo pack up his cart and prepare for a journey. Lorenzo would travel back to the academy and make them see the error of their ways. He would convince them to prepare for the coming of this predicted channeler. He would persuade them they needed to take clairvoyance seriously as a discipline.

"When this new channeler gets to the academy," he said, "we need to be ready to train not just the student's skills, but also their ethics and morals."

Sebastian and Betsy saw Lorenzo off on his journey. He was eager to head to the academy to see if he could change their culture. He said the time spent in the cart on the trip would remind him of his younger days.

* * *

A few days later, Sebastian and Betsy reached the lane that turned off the main road toward Westhavenfieldbrook. Sebastian was very excited to be almost home. It was noon, so the sun was high overhead. Sebastian had hoped to get back a little earlier, but they had been a bit slow getting started this morning.

He saw the stone marker that showed the town name directions. Someone had changed the stone pointing toward Westhavenfieldbrook. Someone had replaced it with a much shorter stone that just read "Hero." Sebastian wasn't exactly sure what to make of this. He looked around to see if they were in the right place. Everything else looked the same, except for that stone.

He pulled on Betsy's lead and headed down the lane toward his village.

60

Rose and Anise stood on both sides of the lane leading out of the village outside the rebuilt town gate. They had been waiting there for hours. Rose was trying to convince Anise that it was time for them to go home.

"Anise," Rose said, "I don't think he's coming today."

"Aunt Rose," said Anise with a quaver in her voice, "I told you. He is."

A banner lay on the dirt of the lane between them. Anise held the cord attached to the top of one side, and Rose had the one attached to the other. The writing couldn't be read at the moment as the written side was face down.

"Anise," said Rose with parental patience in her voice, which somehow had crept in there in the last few weeks, "everyone thinks it's great how much you care about Sebastian's quest, but...."

"There he is!" called out Anise. She jerked on her end of the cord to lift the banner so quickly that the other end was almost pulled out of Rose's hand.

When Rose lifted her end of the cord, the sign rose off the ground. She looked down the lane.

Anise was right. Sebastian and Betsy were headed toward them. She saw the conquering hero, who seemed like a tired and dusty young man to her. She looked over at her niece. Anise's eyes shone through the swollen cheeks and dried tear tracks. Rose wondered what she saw.

Anise held her cord as high as she could. She had her arm up-stretched over her head. The top of her side of the banner was just about at Betsy's nose. The banner read, "Welcome home to Hero, Hero!" The mayor had had several banners and other signs made up. He was planning a welcome home parade.

Betsy walked up to the banner. She sniffed it to see if it was something to eat.

"Anise, Rose," said Sebastian. "It's good to see you."

Anise dropped the cord, ran over to Sebastian, and wrapped her arms around him.

"I'm sorry, Sebastian," she said, crying again. "I'm sorry, it's just us. They wouldn't believe me when I said you were coming today."

Betsy gave up trying to eat the banner and started sniffing at Anise, who had a carrot stashed in her smock.

"Thank you, Anise," said Sebastian, giving Anise a big hug. "I couldn't imagine a nicer welcome home."

61

The following morning Sebastian awoke to a pounding on his door. Somehow the night before, he had managed to avoid getting too much attention. This morning wouldn't be as easy.

When Sebastian made his way to the door to open it, he found the mayor waiting for him.

"You don't look ready, my boy," said the mayor.

"Ready for what?"

"The parade! Your welcome home parade. You need to get dressed, my boy. Don't forget your shield and sword."

While Sebastian was getting ready, the mayor gave him a pep talk to get him excited for the parade. It quickly became apparent this event wasn't about Sebastian for the mayor but about finishing the adventure and the story for the tourism industry, which would put the town of Hero on the map.

When Sebastian and the mayor stepped out the door, a cart was in front of the house. It was a hay cart, with the sides removed. There were banners attached to both sides of the base of the cart. The phrase "The hero of Hero" was written on both.

"I'm not getting on that thing!" said Sebastian.

With talk of his civic responsibilities, how it was for the town, and not for himself, the mayor convinced Sebastian to stand on the back of the cart. The mayor had gotten Mr. Thatcher to lead the horse pulling the wagon. He had recruited Mr. Arkwright, who fancied himself a musician, to play the bagpipes to lead the parade with music. Mr. Arkwright was a masterful piper if you judged the quality of the music purely by the volume. His son Marcus came up with a drum and tried to find the rhythm in the tunes his father belted out.

The mayor had two young daughters and a son. He had

dressed them in their market day best and given each of the girls a basket of flower pedals. The parade started out with the two girls in the front, scattering the petals. The son followed the girls, looking uncomfortable in his Sunday best.

Mr. Arkwright started into his first tune. Marcus bravely attempted to locate the appropriate places to bang on his drum. The parade turned onto Main Street and headed toward the market square.

Sebastian was having difficulty finding a place to hide on the back of the hay cart. It was early enough that some village roosters hadn't started crowing yet. It mortified Sebastian that his reintroduction to his fellow villagers would be waking them up with this unholy racket early in the morning.

As the cart drove slowly down Main Street, the villagers came out of their houses. To Sebastian's surprise, the reaction seemed to be mainly positive. Instead of yelling about the noise, most people coming out of their homes seemed in good spirits. They started following the cart down Main Street.

By the time the cart approached the market square, the parade felt different. The flower petals the girls scattered were shining colorfully in the morning sunshine. Most of the village's population walked down the street behind the cart, murmuring and talking among themselves.

Even Mr. Arkwright seemed to have taken inspiration from his first voluntary and perhaps most appreciative audience ever. For the first time, you could describe his play by other adjectives than just "loud." Marcus seemed to have figured out how to find the beat in his father's tunes.

The parade pulled into the market square. On the opposite side of the cobbles was a large object covered in canvas with a temporary-looking wooden platform standing next to it. Mr. Thatcher pulled the cart up next to the wooden platform, and Sebastian stepped off the wagon onto the platform. The mayor climbed up the slightly rickety wooden stairs on the platform's side to stand next to Sebastian.

The villagers spread out into the market square. Sebastian

scanned through the crowd, picking out Isabel and her mother and then Rose and Anise.

The mayor looked out over the crowd and, in his best "addressing a crowd" voice, called out, "May I present, Sebastian! The hero of Hero!"

62

There was a roar of applause from the crowd. This was almost entirely the same group of people who had been standing here when Sebastian fought the beast. He flushed and felt overcome with gratitude himself. The sense that the people of his village appreciated and valued him made him feel warm all over.

"Speech!" came a cry from the crowd. Soon, it was echoing all over the square.

The mayor stepped forward and started to speak.

"Not you!" came a loud voice from somewhere in the crowd.

The mayor looked skeptical, trying to spot who had called out, but he stepped back.

After a few more cries of "Speech!", and the mayor pushing him forward, Sebastian stepped to the platform's railing.

His first reaction was he couldn't speak to so many people, even though he knew them all. But he grabbed the bottom edge of Gerard's shirt with both hands, tugged it down, so the front of the shirt tightened across his chest, and pulled himself together.

"Thank you," he said. Sebastian tried to raise his voice to a crowd addressing volume as the mayor had. The height of the platform helped a bit.

"As some of you know, I left the village to find out where the creature that attacked us came from and see if there would be more attacks."

Some crowd members started murmuring, and several leaned forward in anticipation.

"You'll be glad to hear I found out where it came from, and I was able to stop it. We should not be attacked again."

There was a roar from the crowd, and someone started

chanting Sebastian's name. He stepped back from the railing, flushing red with embarrassment.

The mayor stepped forward. This time when he started to speak, there were no interruptions.

"You've heard him," he said. "Our hero of Hero has saved us again!"

The mayor paused for a moment as the crowd applauded and then continued. "Our newly renamed town of Hero will forever remember the brave actions of our heroic son," and here he clapped Sebastian on the shoulder to more applause.

"And, to ensure we never forget," the mayor paused dramatically. He gestured to Mr. Arkwright, who had put down his bagpipe and stood near the sizable canvas tarp-covered object, a cord in his hands.

Mr. Arkwright gave the cord a sharp tug. Nothing happened. The mayor made a panicked gesture with his hand as Mr. Arkwright looked over at him to see what he should do. Mr. Arkwright reached over and grabbed the heavy canvas covering the large object with his hands and tried to move it.

The canvas was hardly moving. Some crowd members joined in, and with several hands helping, the tarp finally dropped off the object. Many of the cobblestones formerly hidden by the canvas were stained blue.

It was a large stone obelisk with a metal plaque embedded in it. Sebastian couldn't read it from where he stood, but the mayor resumed talking, and Sebastian was sure the gist of what was written on the plaque would be in what he was saying. Sebastian was enormously relieved what was revealed wasn't a statue. A historical marker he could deal with. A statue of himself would have been a new nightmare.

"On this spot," the mayor intoned. "Sebastian, the Knight of Moon and Shadow, defeated a nightmare creature which threatened to destroy the town of Hero. This creature had already destroyed the village of Anesbury, and Sebastian defeated it in single combat.

"Paraphrased a bit," said the mayor, "but there it is.

"Let's show our hero what we think of him.
"Hip, Hip, Hooray!"
The crowd joined in.
"Hip, Hip, Hooray!"

63

The following morning Sebastian got up early. He finished his morning chores as quickly as possible, as he still had some unfinished business. As he stepped out his front door to get started, Anise, waiting for him, pounced.

"Anise," said Sebastian, "I've got things to do this morning." He held a folded piece of white-colored fabric in his hands.

"I want to help," said Anise.

Sebastian thought about it for a moment. He'd been used to being alone most of his life. Especially since his father died. He'd been planning to finish this quest by himself today. He realized he didn't mind having Anise tagging along. In fact, he thought he liked it.

"I'm not sure I know how to do this myself," said Sebastian.

"Then, we'll learn it together."

Sebastian set off down the lane, with Anise trailing after.

Anise skipped and bounced as they walked through the village, practically bubbling over with delight.

"Which one is first, Sebastian?" she said.

Sebastian held out the folded white fabric he held in his hands.

Sebastian and Anise turned off Main Street onto Blackbird lane.

"When are you going to ask Isabel to marry you?" said Anise.

"What?" said Sebastian, eloquently.

"Are you going to ask her today, or are you going to ask her after you give her shadows back to her?"

"Who told you I was going to ask her at all?" said Sebastian.

"No one told me. I figured it out by myself. Isabel said it was all right, though."

"Isabel said it was all right?" said Sebastian.

They were approaching the Widow Clark's house. Pico's dog house was in the side yard. There was a fence around the yard, but it was always in a state of disrepair. The same people who speculated that the Widow Clark wanted Pico free for additional security thought she kept the fence poorly repaired on purpose so Pico could get out.

The opening in the fence was big enough that Sebastian and Anise could climb through. They hadn't seen any signs of Pico. Anise told Sebastian nobody saw Pico much. He'd been very withdrawn since he'd been silenced.

Sebastian stepped up to the doghouse and leaned over to look inside. It was dark in there, but he thought he saw Pico curled up in the back of the house. He pulled the white fabric, the Pants of the Wind, from his belt.

Anise reached over and grabbed the pants out of Sebastian's hands. "Let me," she said.

"Be careful," said Sebastian. "We're not sure how he'll react."

Anise walked over to the doghouse door and looked in. She could see Pico at the back. He looked at her and tried to whine. Anise partly unfolded the pants and waved them in front of the door opening of the doghouse.

Pico came charging out and started bouncing up and down in front of Sebastian and Anise. He looked for all the world like he had just been offered the biggest treat a dog could imagine. It was strange to see the large dog making excited barking motions but not a sound. Sebastian thought that if Pico had embraced his change, he could have been the terror of all the cats in the neighborhood, sneaking up on them entirely silently.

Anise held the white fabric out to Pico while putting her hand on his head, trying to calm him. Pico opened his mouth, and the material seemed to flow down his throat. It wasn't that Pico ate the fabric. Instead, it seemed to turn to wind and blew down his gullet.

The fabric disappeared instantly, and Pico barked excitedly. His tail wagged like a metronome, and he started licking Anise's face, almost knocking her down in his excitement.

Pico headed back into his doghouse. As Sebastian and Anise turned to leave, they heard joyful grunting noises coming through the door opening.

"Well," said Sebastian, "that seems to have been successful."

64

Sebastian's next visit was to the mayor. He had had difficulty deciding what to do with Leonard's cap. He couldn't return it to Leonard, as Leonard had left town. Sebastian had heard that he was all right, but there wasn't any word of when, or if, he was planning to come back. Also, Sebastian thought that the giving of Leonard's cap had been a blessing for Leonard, as well as being a gift for Sebastian.

Sebastian had given it a great deal of thought, and he concluded that in some ways, the mayor was the kind of a fool who is a fool because he's not enough of a fool. If he were to put the cap on, he would become more foolish, which would allow him to take his foolishness less foolishly.

Sebastian left Blackbird lane and headed back down Main Street toward Market Square. Anise was still close on his tail.

"Anise," said Sebastian, "you don't have to stay with me all day. I've got a lot to do today."

"I know I don't have to," said Anise. "I want to."

Sebastian and Anise entered Market Square and started toward the town hall.

"You said something about Isabel saying it was all right for me to ask her to marry me?" said Sebastian.

"Yes," said Anise. "She also said that you couldn't get married because she kissed you when you left town. Or something like that. But I think you should ask her anyway."

Sebastian felt like he was getting whiplash. They approached the main door of the town hall. Sebastian opened the door, and they entered.

Mary, the miller's second daughter, was working as the town hall assistant today. Mr. Shepherd, the miller, was trying to curry favor with the mayor, so he'd been asking his daughters to volunteer. He was trying to get the mayor to appoint him and his family the official village bakers. Unfortunately for Mr. Shepherd, the mayor had secretly grown very fond of Rose's lemon custard tarts.

Mary greeted Sebastian and Anise with a friendly smile. She nodded to Anise, who she had seen around town.

"Good morning. How can I help you today?" Mary said very officially. She'd been practicing her official greeting. She'd just said the same thing to the empty room several times before they walked in.

"I was hoping to see the mayor," said Sebastian.

"Just a moment," said Mary. "I'll check to see if he's in." Mary knew quite well that the mayor was in. He had the habit of bouncing a ball off his office wall when he was bored. She could hear the regular thumping of the ball hitting the wall. It wasn't loud enough to be distracting unless you knew what it was.

Mary got up and knocked on the door of the mayor's office. She stuck her head in, and Sebastian and Anise heard a quiet conversation. Mary stepped back to her desk and gestured them toward the door.

The door opened as they approached it, and the mayor came out. He clasped Sebastian's hand in both his hands and shook it vigorously up and down.

"Sebastian, my boy," he said, "I've always got time for the hero of Hero. What can I do for you today?"

"I'm hoping it's more what I can do for you, Mr. Mayor," said Sebastian.

The mayor looked at Sebastian inquiringly.

Sebastian pulled Leonard's cap from his belt. "Mr. Mayor," he said, "as you know, this is part of the armor of the Knight of Moon and Shadow. I want to present it to you for the official use of the office of mayor of this village."

The mayor looked slightly irked. "Town," he muttered under his breath.

"As you may not know," Sebastian continued, "when I put this cap on during the battle with the nightmare which attacked this town, it gave me courage."

"Of course, I'm honored," said the mayor, "but in most of the situations I have to deal with daily, courage isn't an attribute I need."

"And," said Sebastian, "it's not exactly what you would get from wearing this cap."

The mayor waited expectantly for Sebastian to continue.

"What I believe wearing this cap will give you is a change in perspective. I would recommend putting this cap on when you have to make critical decisions. It should help you form wise opinions about difficult questions.

"A couple of additional pieces of advice about how to use this powerful item," Sebastian continued. "You should not wear it unless you're imminently about to make a decision, and you should remove it immediately when you're done."

The mayor reached out carefully and took the cap from Sebastian's hand. "I'll take that under advisement. Thank you, Sebastian," said the mayor.

65

Sebastian knocked on the door of the Fletcher family's house. Anise stood behind him. Above his head, hanging over the door frame, was a large wooden pair of shoes. The shoes were there to mark this as the home and place of business of a cobbler.

The door opened, and Mrs. Fletcher stuck her head out. She took one look at Sebastian and said, "What do *you* want?"

"Good afternoon, Mrs. Fletcher," said Sebastian. "Is Gerard at home?"

"He is," said Mrs. Fletcher, "he always is, recently. But I'm not sure I want you to see him."

"Mrs. Fletcher," said Sebastian, trying to put on his most winning tone. "I need to talk to Gerard for a moment. I borrowed something of his which I need to return."

"He'll feel better," said Anise from behind Sebastian.

Mrs. Fletcher reluctantly opened the door and led them up a narrow flight of stairs. The Fletcher family lived on the second floor above Mr. Fletcher's workshop.

She knocked on a door and opened it without waiting for an answer. She stuck her head in, and Sebastian and Anise heard a mumbled conversation. Mrs. Fletcher opened the door wider and stepped to one side so they could walk in.

Gerard was lying on his bed on one side of the room. On the opposite side was a large open wardrobe. There were several nice-looking pairs of shoes littering the dresser's floor. Some glamorous clothes were hanging inside. However, they weren't arranged as nicely as they might have been, and a few expensive shirts lay casually on the floor.

Gerard was wearing a simple cotton nightshirt and looked tired and sad.

Sebastian went over to where Gerard was lying. Gerard rose to his feet. Sebastian said, "Gerard, I am grateful to you for your gift."

"Thank you, Sebastian," said Gerard.

"I've come to give you your shirt back."

Gerard took a step back and raised one hand, palm outward. "No, thank you," he said. "I may be a little sad now, but I don't like who I was when I wore that."

"It's all right, Gerald," said Sebastian. "It won't be the same, I promise."

Sebastian held the shirt out toward Gerard. It still seemed to glow bright with color. The place where it had ripped in the battle with the beast and Sebastian had sewn it up was clearly visible.

"Are you sure, Sebastian?" said Gerard. "I like plain simple things now. I don't want to stick out."

"Look at it, Gerard," said Sebastian, gesturing toward the shirt and almost incidentally toward the mended tear. "It's not the same as it was."

Gerard took the shirt carefully. He put it on over his nightshirt. As it settled down over his shoulders, he seemed to stand a little straighter and taller than he had.

Sebastian reached out and clapped Gerard on the back. "How does it feel?" he asked.

Gerard stood up even a little straighter and shook Sebastian's hand. "It feels good," he said. "I feel good." The handshake with Sebastian grew firmer as he spoke.

"Thank you, Sebastian," he said. "And I don't just mean for the shirt. Thank you for what you have done for the village as well."

66

Sebastian and Anise had just one more stop. As they headed down the street toward the Fisher house, Sebastian felt nervous for the first time that day. Until now, everything they were doing was quest business. The Knight of Moon and Shadow had taken care of it. This next errand felt more personal.

The small-scaled wooden cabinet hanging over the door frame to the Fisher's carpentry shop swung a bit as the door opened, and Mrs. Fisher and Isabel stepped out. They started walking down the street away from Sebastian and Anise.

"Mrs. Fisher, Isabel!" called out Sebastian, speeding up his pace toward them. Anise struggled to keep up.

The sun was setting behind them as Mrs. Fisher and Isabel turned to see who was hailing them. The setting sun's rays shone straight through Isabel's feet as they stubbornly refused to cast shadows.

"Sebastian," said Isabel, a little breathlessly.

"Isabel," said Sebastian, "I have something of yours." He pulled the shapeless dark shadows folded over his belt out and held them in his hand.

Isabel and Mrs. Fisher waited a second for Sebastian and Anise to approach. As soon as they were close enough, Sebastian dropped to one knee in front of Isabel.

"Not this again," said Mrs. Fisher, with a smile.

Sebastian reached out with one of the dark shapes in his hand and gently held Isabel's ankle. There was a small amount of pressure as he massaged the substance into her calf and foot. Sebastian took the second shape and, holding it in one hand, pinched a small amount of the dark material off of it. Then he massaged the second shadow into Isabel's other calf and foot.

Isabel's shadow now showed her feet and ankles as it

stretched across the ground. Sebastian took the slight pinch of material he held in his hand and worked it with his fingers for a moment.

Still on one knee in front of Isabel, Sebastian turned his face up to her. He held a small dark object out toward her and said, "Isabel Fisher, will you marry me?"

Anise clapped. Isabel looked at the object in Sebastian's hand. It was a small dark ring, woven of material that looked at the same time substantial and also wispy like it could blow away at any moment.

* * *

Now, suppose you're worried Sebastian made the ring out of part of the shadow of Isabel's feet, leaving her still incomplete. In that case, you'll be happy to know that he used the shadow cast by the shoes Isabel was wearing that day. Those shoes were still lying sadly shadow-less in Isabel's closet.

67

A few days later, on a night when the moon would have been full had it been in its usual place, Sebastian went out to Swenson's cow pasture. The moon obviously was not in the sky, as Sebastian had it with him. He held it in front of himself, lighting the way as he walked through the field toward the back fence.

Sebastian had to weave a bit as he walked to avoid the cow patties. The Swensons kept more cattle in this relatively small field than Sebastian liked. He preferred to give the cows as much room to roam as possible. The bright light from the moon in his hands made navigation easy.

Sebastian reached the back fence and climbed up. The climbing was awkward with the moon in his hands, but he got up on the crossbar just below the top. He gave the moon a kiss for good luck, held it up as high as possible, and jumped.

There was a clank as the edge of the moon thudded against something in the sky, but nothing held, and Sebastian and the moon wound up lying on the grass of the Swenson's field. Sebastian landed with a cow patty just a few inches in front of his face. He thanked his lucky stars and perhaps the little kiss he had given the moon that it hadn't been closer.

He got up and climbed back up onto the fence. This time, he made an effort to climb to the very top. The balancing act of standing on the very top of the top crossbar while holding the moon was challenging. It helped that he didn't have to stay long once he got there but could immediately take a leap upward.

Sebastian jumped and felt the moon collide with something invisible above him. There was a satisfying click, and the moon latched into place. Sebastian hung for a second, holding onto the moon's lower edge. For a moment, he was reluctant to let go. It had felt magical and unique being the Knight of Moon and Shadow. He wasn't sure he was ready to return to being just Sebastian, the farmer again. Then he remembered Isabel's answer to his question from a couple of days before, and he smiled.

Sebastian let go of the moon and dropped to the grass, narrowly missing another of the Swenson's cow pies. Just as it was time to let go of the moon, it was time to let go of the Knight of Moon and Shadow.

The full moon's bright light lit Sebastian's path as he made his way from Swenson's pasture back home.

EPILOGUE

That summer, Isabel Fisher and Sebastian were married. Anise was the ring bearer. She was very proud to bear the ring, which she immediately named "The Ring of Shadow." The whole village came to the wedding. The mayor made sure it was a spectacle that added to the tourist reputation of the town.

The mayor appointed Rose the official town baker, with the condition that the town hall would be well supplied with lemon custard tarts. Mr. Shepherd, the miller, was initially indignant at this. But, he had recently discovered Rose's rhubarb pie, so he complained less than he might have.

Anise spent almost as much time at Aunt Isabel and Uncle Sebastian's house as she did at the bakery. Rose wasn't always happy about this, but it seemed Isabel and Sebastian didn't mind, so she let it go.

It wasn't long before Isabel and Sebastian were expecting. They named their first son Twilight and called him Twi for short.

Lilith kept a careful eye on Anise. She knew she had to bring the girl's potential to the academy's attention, but she thought there was no hurry.

* * *

But those are tales for another time.

Dear Reader,

Thank you for reading Moon & Shadow. If you've grown fond of Sebastian and Anise—as I have—you may enjoy continuing their journey in Sun & Dream, where new challenges await at the Academy, and dreams hold more power than anyone realizes.

And if this book brought you joy, I'd be truly grateful if you left a quick review on Amazon. Your words help others discover the story—and help me continue writing them.

Warmly,

J. Steven Lamperti

BOOKS IN THIS SERIES

The Channeler Trilogy

Sun & Dream

Dreams can change the world—if they don't change her first.

Anise has always lived half in dreams. But when she begins her training at the Academy—a hidden school where magic and dreams entwine—her quiet life in the village of Hero fades into memory.

There, among scholars, mages, and strange gods, Anise discovers that her gift for channeling daemons is far greater—and far more dangerous—than she ever imagined.

Whispers swirl through the Academy's halls. Secrets glimmer behind friendly faces. And somewhere between sunlit classrooms and shadowed dreams, Anise must decide who she can trust—including a golden-eyed god who speaks of destiny.

In a world where dreams shape reality, mastering her magic may be the only way to save everything she loves.

Wry, wondrous, and full of quiet peril, Sun & Dream is the second book in the Channeler Trilogy—perfect for fans of Diana Wynne Jones and The Girl Who Drank the Moon.

Death & Dragon

The dream is broken. The world is burning. Anise must find a new way to fight.

Cast into the heart of the dream realm, Anise awakens to a world unraveling. Dragons darken the skies. Nightmares spill into the waking world. And those she once trusted have become strangers.

Armed with her channeler's magic—and guided by an unlikely ally in the god of death—Anise must weave light from shadow before Liamec falls to ruin.

But dreams are tricky things. Old enemies wear new faces. Love and loyalty blur. And at the end of the path waits a sacrifice no magic can undo.

In a battle where dreams shape reality, Anise must decide: What is she willing to lose to save the world she loves?

Epic, heartfelt, and filled with wonder, Death & Dragon is the unforgettable conclusion to the Channeler Trilogy—perfect for fans of Diana Wynne Jones and The Girl Who Drank the Moon.

Perfect for readers who love dream magic, dragon battles, and emotionally rich fantasy finales.

BOOKS BY THIS AUTHOR

The Wolf's Tooth

Twee never chose the wild, but it raised him all the same. After fire scatters his pack, he's swept into a world of outlaws, city streets, and forge smoke. In Grisput, a city that sells its servants and forgets its poor, he learns to work iron—and meets a red-haired street girl with magic in her pockets and more to her past than she lets on.

But whispers of a clairvoyant's prophecy follow him, and the King's Guard has begun to listen.

For readers who love A Wizard of Earthsea and Stardust, The Wolf's Tooth is a warm, wondrous coming-of-age tale about finding kinship in unexpected places—and strength in the quiet heart of a boy who never asked to be special.

Step into the forest. Follow the smoke. The story begins where the wild things run.

Perfect for readers who love quiet heroes, slow-burn wonder, and fantasy that grows from the roots up.

By The Sea

The sea took her brother. Now, it's calling her name.

Years after a storm claimed her brother's life, Annabelle Fisher still walks the shoreline—but she keeps her heart turned away from the sea, and from anyone whose eyes dance with the waves.

When a handsome stranger delivers a formal invitation to a ball at the duke's castle, her carefully quiet life begins to unravel. What begins with a single dance draws her into a world of ancient rivalries and ocean-born secrets.

Beneath the surface lies a mythic realm ruled by gods, where memories twist like currents and love can't be trusted. To protect the family she has left, Annabelle must follow a path that leads through longing, grief—and into the shadowed halls of Hades himself.

Lyrical and sea-swept, By the Sea is a romantic YA fantasy of loss, courage, and ocean magic—perfect for fans of The Scorpio Races and The Girl Who Fell Beneath the Sea.

Twilight's Fall

A quiet guardsman. A fallen king. A kingdom on the edge of ruin.

Corentin never wanted to be a hero. But when an ambush shatters King Twilight's journey home from the far reaches of his realm, he finds himself on the run with the young monarch—and two unexpected allies: Aela, an herbalist with sharp eyes and a steadier heart, and Blaine, a fellow guardsman who escaped the ambush at his side.

As old loyalties crumble and secrets rise from the shadows, Corentin must reckon with a legacy he never asked for—and a power buried deeper than he knows. To protect the king, he'll have to step out of the quiet and into the fight for Liamec's future.

Blending myth, tenderness, and slow-burning romance, Twilight's Fall is a richly woven YA fantasy for fans of The Queen of the Tearling and The Bone Houses.

Perfect for readers who love loyal heroes, quiet strength, and fantasy where friendships matter as much as fate.

Sunshine Over Hero

Strange things are happening in the village of Hero.

First it was the sheep—found drained of blood. Then village girls began to disappear, returning days later with no memory of where they'd been.

Sunny, a sharp-minded farm girl with no patience for nonsense, is sure something unnatural is behind it. But when Raphael shows up—a traveling monster hunter whose last case involved a mouse spirit stealing cheese—she realizes help might not be as heroic as she'd hoped.

Raphael does have a few advantages: a talking silver sword named Cutter, a fire imp named Iggy who only ever says "Burn," and a willingness to follow Sunny's lead. The only problem? Cutter's eloquence and Iggy's enthusiasm don't always mix.

As the mystery deepens, Sunny and Raphael uncover an ancient threat—and an unexpected connection that neither of them saw coming.

The Pirates Of Meara

A silver-eyed girl washes up from the sea, and nothing in Mouse's life is quiet again.

Fern is a duke's daughter, stolen by pirates and cast ashore in a city she doesn't understand.

Mouse is a street orphan who thought he knew Meara—until the city begins whispering secrets only he can hear.

Now the pirate Bluebeard hunts them both. Fern thinks it's for ransom. But the truth runs deeper, hidden in stone and salt.

Because Mouse isn't just a quiet boy with a borrowed name—he's the key to an undersea world, and the city has not forgotten.

The Pirates of Meara is a gentle, magical tale of friendship, lost cities, and the tide that pulls us home—perfect for fans of The Chronicles of Prydain and The True Confessions of Charlotte Doyle.

For readers who love quiet heroes, sea-swept wonder, and cities where the past still stirs.

Endymion And The Fae

A shepherd boy, a girl of the fae, and a love that could heal—or divide—their worlds.

High in the mountain meadows, Endymion tends his sheep where mist clings to the slopes and old songs ride the wind. His life is simple—until he meets Lily, a girl of the Wee Folk with eyes like wildfire and a laugh like spring water.

To her people, she is Wee Folk. To his, she is Fae—a name spoken with fear, as if it carried danger of its own. What begins as a tender bond soon sets two worlds on edge.

When old wounds flare, Endymion must choose between peace and passion, tradition and hope. If he and Lily cannot bridge the divide, their love may cost more than their hearts.

A standalone tale within the Tales of Liamec, Endymion and the Fae is a gentle, slow-burn fantasy romance of first love, meadow magic, and quiet rebellion—for those who cherish cozy folklore, tender magic, and the stillness of high pastures.